PUFFIN BOOKS

The Puffin Book of Stories for Nine-Year-Olds

Wendy Cooling was educated in Norwich and, after a short time in the Civil Service, spent time travelling the world. On her return to England she trained as a teacher, went on to teach English in London comprehensive schools for many years and was for a time seconded as an advisor on libraries and book-related work in schools. She left teaching to work on the promotion of books and reading as Head of The Children's Book Foundation and now works as a freelance book consultant and reviewer.

She writes Children's Guides for the National Trust, and has edited many short story and poetry anthologies, including the millennium collection *Centuries of Stories*.

THE PUFFIN BOOK OF
Stories for Nine-Year-Olds

Edited by Wendy Cooling

Illustrated by Steve Cox

PUFFIN BOOKS

PUFFIN BOOKS

Penguin Books Ltd, 27 Wrights Lane, London W8 5TZ, England
Penguin Putnam Inc., 375 Hudson Street, New York, New York 10014, USA
Penguin Books Australia Ltd, Ringwood, Victoria, Australia
Penguin Books Canada Ltd, 10 Alcorn Avenue, Toronto, Ontario, Canada M4V 3B2
Penguin Books India (P) Ltd, 11 Community Centre, Panchsheel Park,
New Delhi – 110 017, India
Penguin Books (NZ) Ltd, Cnr Rosedale and Airborne Roads, Albany,
Auckland, New Zealand
Penguin Books (South Africa) (Pty) Ltd, 5 Watkins Street, Denver Ext 4,
Johannesburg 2094, South Africa

On the World Wide Web at: www.penguin.com

Penguin Books Ltd, Registered Offices: Harmondsworth, Middlesex, England

First published 2001
1

The moral right of the authors and editor has been asserted

The Acknowledgements on pages 135 to 138 constitute an
extension of this copyright page

Set in Monotype Ehrhardt
Typeset by Rowland Phototypesetting Ltd, Bury St Edmunds, Suffolk
Made and printed in England by Clays Ltd, St Ives plc

British Library Cataloguing in Publication Data
A CIP catalogue record for this book is available from the British Library

ISBN 0–141–30659–9

Contents

Introduction

The stories here range across the world and across history. There are stories for all moods: stories about real situations, stories with a touch of magic and stories to make you laugh. Some tales are traditional and some, although very new, are told in the style of the traditional or folk tale.

This is a collection to dip into rather than to read from beginning to end. Above all, I hope you will enjoy these stories. They will introduce you to some wonderful children's writers.

Wendy Cooling

The Mouth-Organ Boys

JAMES BERRY

I wanted a mouth-organ, I wanted it more than anything else in the whole world. I told my mother. She kept ignoring me, but I still wanted a mouth-organ badly.

I was only a boy. I didn't have a proper job. Going to school was like a job, but nobody paid me to go to school. Again I had to say to my mother, 'Mam, will you please buy a mouth-organ for me?'

It was the first time now that my mother stood and answered me properly. Yet listen to what my mother said. 'What d'you want a mouth-organ for?'

3

'All the other boys have a mouth-organ, Mam,' I told her.

'Why is that so important? You don't have to have something just because others have it.'

'They won't have me with them without a mouth-organ, Mam,' I said.

'They'll soon change their minds, Delroy.'

'They won't, Mam. They really won't. You don't know Wildo Harris. He never changes his mind. And he never lets any other boy change his mind either.'

'Delroy, I haven't got the time to argue with you. There's no money to buy a mouth-organ. I bought your new shoes and clothes for Independence celebrations. Remember?'

'Yes, Mam.'

'Well, money doesn't come on trees.'

'No, Mam.' I had to agree.

'It's a school-day. The sun won't stand still for you. Go and feed the fowls. Afterwards milk the goat. Then get yourself ready for school.'

She sent me off. I had to go and do my morning jobs.

Oh, my mother never listened! She never understood anything. She always had reasons why she couldn't buy me something and it was no good wanting to talk to my dad. He always cleared off to work early.

All my friends had a mouth-organ, Wildo, Jim, Desmond, Len – everybody had one, except me. I couldn't go round with them now. They wouldn't let anybody go round with them without a mouth-organ. They were now 'The Mouth-Organ Boys'. And we used to be all friends. I used to be their friend. We all used to play games together, and have fun together. Now they pushed me away.

'Delroy! Delroy!' my mother called.

I answered loudly. 'Yes, Mam!'

'Why are you taking so long feeding the fowls?'

'Coming, Mam.'

'Hurry up, Delroy.'

Delroy. Delroy. Always calling Delroy!

I milked the goat. I had breakfast. I quickly brushed my teeth. I washed my face and hands and legs. No time left and my mother said nothing about getting my mouth-organ. But my mother had time to grab my head and comb and brush my hair. She had time to wipe away toothpaste from my lip with her hand. I had to pull myself away and say, 'Good day, Mam.'

'Have a good day, Delroy,' she said, staring at me.

I ran all the way to school. I ran wondering if the

Mouth-Organ Boys would let me sit with them today. Yesterday they didn't sit next to me in class.

I was glad the boys came back. We all sat together as usual. But they teased me about not having a mouth-organ.

Our teacher, Mr Goodall, started writing on the blackboard. Everybody was whispering. And it got to everybody talking quite loudly. Mr Goodall could be really cross. Mr Goodall had big muscles. He had a moustache too. I would like to be like Mr Goodall when I grow up. But he could be really cross. Suddenly Mr Goodall turned round and all the talking stopped, except for the voice of Wildo Harris. Mr Goodall held the chalk in his hand and stared at Wildo Harris – he looked at Teacher and dried up. The whole class giggled.

Mr Goodall picked out Wildo Harris for a question. He stayed sitting and answered.

'Will you please stand up when you answer a question?' Mr Goodall said.

Wildo stood up and answered again. Mr Goodall ignored him and asked another question. Nobody answered. Mr Goodall pointed at me and called my name. I didn't know why he picked on me. I didn't know I knew the answer. I wanted to stand up slowly, to kill time. But I was there, standing. I gave an answer.

'That is correct,' Mr Goodall said.

I sat down. My forehead felt hot and sweaty, but I felt good. Then in the school yard at recess time, Wildo joked about it. Listen to what he had to say: 'Delroy Brown isn't only a big head. Delroy Brown can answer questions with a big mouth.'

'Yeah!' the gang roared, to tease me.

Then Wildo had to say, 'If only he could get a *mouth*-organ.' All the boys laughed and walked away.

I went home to lunch and as usual I came back quickly. Wildo and Jim and Desmond and Len were together, at the bench, under the palm tree. I went up to them. They were swapping mouth-organs, trying out each one. Everybody made sounds on each mouth-organ, and said something. I begged Len, I begged Desmond, I begged Jim, to let me try out their mouth-organs. I only wanted a blow. They just carried on making silly sounds on each other's mouth-organs. I begged Wildo to lend me his. He didn't even look at me.

I faced Wildo. I said, 'Look. I can do something different as a Mouth-Organ Boy. Will you let me do something different?'

Boy, everybody was interested. Everybody looked at me.

'What different?' Wildo asked.

'I can play the comb,' I said.

'Oh, yeah?' Wildo said slowly.

'Want to hear it?' I asked. 'My dad taught me how to play it.'

'Yeah,' Wildo said. 'Let's hear it.' And not one boy smiled or anything. They just waited.

I took out my comb. I put my piece of tissue-paper over it. I began to blow a tune on my comb and had to stop. The boys were laughing too much. They laughed so much they staggered about. Other children came up and laughed too. It was all silly, laughing at me.

I became angry. Anybody would get mad. I told them they could keep their silly Mouth-Organ Boys' business. I told them it only happened because Desmond's granny gave him a mouth-organ for his birthday. And it only caught on because Wildo went and got a mouth-organ too. I didn't sit with the boys in class that afternoon. I didn't care what the boys did.

I went home. I looked after my goats. Then I ate. I told my mum I was going for a walk. I went into the centre of town where I had a great surprise.

The boys were playing mouth-organs and dancing. They played and danced in the town square. Lots of kids followed the boys and danced around them.

It was great. All four boys had the name 'The

Mouth-Organ Boys' across their chests. It seemed they did the name themselves. They cut out big coloured letters for the words from newspapers and magazines. They gummed the letters down on a strip of brown paper, then they made a hole at each end of the paper. Next a string was pushed through the holes, so they could tie the names round them. The boys looked great. What a super name: 'The Mouth-Organ Boys'! How could they do it without me!

'Hey, boys!' I shouted, and waved. 'Hey, boys!' They saw me. They jumped up more with a bigger act, but ignored me. I couldn't believe Wildo, Jim, Desmond and Len enjoyed themselves so much and didn't care about me.

I was sad, but I didn't follow them. I hung about the garden railings, watching. Suddenly I didn't want to watch any more. I went home slowly. It made me sick how I didn't have a mouth-organ. I didn't want to eat. I didn't want the lemonade and bun my mum gave me. I went to bed.

Mum thought I wasn't well. She came to see me. I didn't want any fussing about. I shut my eyes quickly. She didn't want to disturb me. She left me alone. I opened my eyes again.

If I could drive a truck I could buy loads of mouth-organs. If I was a fisherman I could buy a hundred mouth-organs. If I was an aeroplane pilot I could buy truck-loads of mouth-organs. I was thinking all those things and didn't know when I fell asleep.

Next day at school the Mouth-Organ Boys sat with me. I didn't know why, but we just sat together and joked a little bit. I felt good running home to lunch in the usual bright sunlight.

I ran back to school. The Mouth-Organ Boys were under the palm tree, on the bench. I was really happy. They were really unhappy and cross and this was very strange.

Wildo grabbed me and held me tight. 'You thief!' he said.

The other boys came around me. 'Let's search him,' they said.

'No, no!' I said. 'No.'

'I've lost my mouth-organ and you have stolen it,' Wildo said.

'No,' I said. 'No.'

'What's bulging in your pocket then?'

'It's mine,' I told them. 'It's mine.'

The boys held me. They took the mouth-organ from my pocket.

'It's mine,' I said. But I saw myself going up to Headmaster. I saw myself getting caned. I saw myself disgraced.

Wildo held up the mouth-organ. 'Isn't this red mouth-organ mine?'

'Of course it is,' the boys said.

'It's mine,' I said. 'I got it at lunchtime.'

'Just at the right time, eh?' Desmond said.

'Say you borrowed it,' Jim said.

'Say you were going to give it back,' Len said.

Oh, I had to get a mouth-organ just when Wildo lost his! 'My mother gave it to me at lunchtime,' I said.

'Well, come and tell teacher,' Wildo said.

The bell rang. We hurried to our class. My head was aching. My hands were sweating. My mother would have to come to school, and I hated that.

Wildo told our teacher I stole his mouth-organ. It was no good telling Teacher it was mine, but I did. Wildo said his mouth-organ was exactly like that. And I didn't have a mouth-organ.

Mr Goodall went to his desk. And Mr Goodall brought back Wildo's grubby red mouth-organ. He said it was found on the floor.

How could Wildo compare his dirty red mouth-organ with my new, my beautiful, my shining-clean mouth-organ? Mr Goodall made Wildo Harris say he was sorry.

Oh it was good. It was good to become one of 'The Mouth-Organ Boys'.

What's in a Name?

MARY ROSS

Roz glared at her mother. 'There's not even a decent ice-rink,' she stormed. 'What about all the competitions and things? I'll never be able to enter them now we're here.'

Mrs Tompkin looked up from the newspaper. 'Don't keep on, Roz. What did you expect us to do – stay in London and let your father live in digs?'

'He could have turned it down,' Roz muttered beneath her breath.

'Give up, kid.' Her brother gave her a warning

glance. 'Mum and Dad have got enough to worry about without you wittering on all the time.'

Roz subsided into sulky silence. It's all right for Tony, she thought. He's away at college. It's me that has to live here.

Yesterday had been her first day at the new school, and it had been awful. Absolutely foul. She had got lost about a million times, and every time she went to sit down somebody would say, 'Sorry, I'm keeping that for Gillian,' or Debbie, or some other stuck-up pig. And as for the teachers!

'Name please,' the form teacher had said.

'Roz. Roz Tompkin.'

'Roz? How do you spell it?'

'R . . . O . . . Z.'

'Is that your full name?'

All eyes were on her. She felt herself going red. 'It's short for Rosanne,' she said, 'but everyone calls me Roz.'

'Do they indeed?'

'Yes, they do,' she said defiantly.

The teacher looked up sharply, her lips tightening. For a moment Roz thought she had gone too far. But then the teacher looked back down at the register and the moment had passed.

A girl in the front row turned round, her eyes hard

as burnt currants. Her mouth curved in a knowing smirk, and Roz saw her nudge the girl next to her.

At break, a group of them gathered round her. 'Hey, what's your name?' Burnt Currants asked. 'What's the A stand for?'

'The A?' Startled, Roz swung round to face her.

'It's on a name tag, sticking out of the back of your shirt. R. A. Tompkin. What you got a name tag for? Couldn't you remember your own name?'

Roz flushed painfully. She'd been a weekly boarder at the other school and everything had to be labelled. Why hadn't she remembered to cut it off?

'R. A. Tompkin,' Burnt Currants said again. 'You know what that spells? RAT!'

Suddenly they formed a circle round her, chanting, 'Ratty, Ratty. She's going babby.'

Nearer and nearer they came, menacing her with leering faces. Roz bit her lip. There was no way she'd tell them what the A stood for. Maybe she could force her way out of the circle? Hit one of them in the teeth? Kick her way out? She clenched her fist in readiness . . .

Dring . . . dring. The shrill note of the school bell cut through her thoughts and the circle drifted away like magic as everyone crowded towards the doors.

A slim Asian girl smiled at her as they walked back

into the classroom. 'Don't worry about Louise,' she whispered. 'She's like this with all the new girls.'

After lunch there was a note on the register. Puzzled, the teacher read it. 'Does anyone know anything about this?' she enquired, holding it up.

'No, Miss Jenkyns,' the class chorused.

The teacher sighed. 'Stand up, Rosanne,' she said.

Thirty pairs of eyes swivelled round to look at her.

Miss Jenkyns paused. She knew exactly how long to time it for the most effect. Taking off her spectacles, she put them carefully down on the register. 'I thought I asked you this morning what was your full name. Perhaps I forgot? Or perhaps you didn't hear me?'

The silence seemed to go on for ever.

'Well?'

'I heard you, miss.'

It was like a cat playing with a mouse. The voice was still silky smooth. 'Perhaps you didn't understand. Would anyone like to explain what "full name" means?'

A hand shot up in the air. Roz didn't need to look. She knew exactly whose hand it was.

'Please, miss.' The hand waggled importantly.

'Ah. I thought it might be you, Louise.'

'Full name means the complete name . . . all of it . . .' The voice gloated in its power.

'Thank you.' The teacher's gaze returned to her victim. 'Now, would you please give me your full name – including your middle name.'

'Rosanne Andrianov Tompkin.'

The explosion of laughter was quickly stifled as the teacher tapped her pen on the desk. 'Enough! Andrianov? How do you spell it?'

Roz told her.

'In future, when I ask a question, I expect a truthful answer. Understand?'

Roz nodded miserably.

'And Louise?'

'Yes, miss?' Louise glowed with triumph.

'If I need help with my register or anything else, I will ask for it. Is that understood?'

Louise glared at Roz before lowering her eyes. 'Yes, miss.'

When she got home Roz flung her bag down in a corner and slammed the front door. 'Was it that bad?' She felt her mother's hand on her shoulder.

'Yes it was,' she fumed. 'They called me Ratty again. Just like they did in the last school.'

Her mother tried to put an arm round her, but Roz

shrugged it away. There was a pause, then her mother said gently, 'Your father went back to Richmond today – to the ice-rink. He's arranged for you to take up your ice-skating lessons again. It's only an hour on the motorway, so I'll be able to take you in the car most times. If I can't you'll have to go by train. It'll mean getting up very early on Mondays and Fridays – but I don't suppose you'll mind?'

Anger forgotten, Roz flung her arms round her mother. 'Brilliant. Thanks, Mum. That'll be great.'

After that first week the new school didn't seem so bad. Roz made a few friends and now that she was back ice-skating nothing else mattered. Louise soon found someone else to bully and left her alone – though the nickname stuck, worse luck.

'You were lucky,' her new friend Sula said. 'Last year, on Sports Day, Louise and a couple of her pals were going to beat me up after school just because I was faster than her in the one hundred metres race.'

Roz stared at her. 'And did she?'

Sula shook her head. 'No fear. I came second in the next race. I'm not stupid.'

'You mean you ducked it, just because Louise threatened you?'

Sula flushed. 'What else could I do?'

'But surely if the rest of you stuck together?' Her voice trailed away. What was the use? If nobody had managed to get their own back up to now, what chance would she have?

They were practising hard at Richmond for the Inter-club Competitions. Roz knew that she had a good chance of winning her section in the free skating, and she was looking forward to it, but she was looking forward even more to what came after . . . The last part of the programme was a show-skating exhibition by the home team, and she and Tony had worked out a clown routine that had the rest of them in stitches.

'Honestly, it's brilliant,' she told Sula. 'I didn't think Tony would be able to take part this year – with going to college and everything, but it's only a bus ride away so I've seen more of him this term than I did when we were *living* in London.'

She didn't tell any of the others about her ice-skating. Well, if Louise and her lot heard about it they'd make her life a misery, wouldn't they? But then Miss Jenkyns, the form teacher, said that they would be going up to Richmond to watch the competitions . . .

'A coach will pick us up outside the school gates at ten o'clock,' Miss Jenkyns said. 'I'm told that Louise is one of our most promising skaters. I hope that as many of you as possible will support her.'

On Thursday, Miss Jenkyns collected the money from those who were going on the trip. When she got to the Ts in the register she paused.

'Rosanne Tompkin?' She had never got round to calling her Roz, but at least nobody laughed at it any more.

'No, miss,' Roz stammered. 'That is, yes, miss. But I'm going with my mum in the car. I'm in them.'

'In the competitions?'

Everyone's eyes were on her. 'Yes, miss, I go skating twice a week – before I come to school.'

The teacher's eyes were reflective. She looked as though she were searching her memory for something . . . 'I see. Well, this will make it even more interesting, won't it, Louise?' But Louise only glared.

The class were already taking up most of the front row and talking excitedly by the time Roz and her mother arrived. Sula looked round and waved, but no one else seemed to notice her. For the first time Roz felt self-conscious. Don't let anything go wrong, she thought, crossing her fingers. Don't let me fall on that double axel. Not right at the beginning of the routine. It wouldn't matter so much on the combination . . .

well, it would of course. But if she fell at the beginning it would put her off for the rest of the routine.

'Is that your class?' her mother asked. 'Aren't you going round to talk to them?'

'No. I feel embarrassed.'

'Embarrassed? I've never heard you say that before.' Her mother looked at her thoughtfully. 'You haven't told them, have you? Why not?'

Roz shrugged.

'Embarrassed about me? Because I used to be a famous skater?'

Roz felt a tell-tale blush spread up her neck.

At that moment they were called to warm up for the Free section, and she saw Louise take off her skate guards and thrust forward on to the ice. With thudding heart and tense muscles, Roz peeled off her anorak and followed her.

Louise was just taking off in a double toe loop when she saw Roz. For a split second she seemed to hang in the air before completely losing her balance and landing in an untidy heap on the ice. Grinning to herself, Roz skated past and into a three jump. As she landed she caught a glimpse of Louise's face.

'I'll get you, Ratty,' the girl hissed.

Roz giggled. 'You watch I don't get you first.'

20

The minute's warm-up sped past as she relaxed into the familiar spirals, jumps and arabesques. *I wish I was on after Louise instead of before*, she thought. There wasn't much chance to judge the other girl's standard when they were both skating. There would be no chance to see what Louise was like until after her own performance was finished.

'Clear the ice please.'

As she skated back to the barrier Roz noticed that her brother had arrived and was sitting next to her mother. *Good*. Tony wasn't as critical of her skating as Mum was. Still, it was her mother's opinion she really valued.

A slight click signalled the beginning of the tape for the first competitor's music. Roz recognized the overture to *Aspects of Love*. It was a piece that she had nearly chosen herself. She was so glad now that she'd had second thoughts.

The music faded away leaving the skater in a deep lunge, her arms draped over the forward leg. She stood up with a look of relief on her face and skated back to the barrier.

After a pause the marks were called out. '3·5, 3·6, 3·2, 3·5.' Then for Artistic Impression. '3·4, 3·5, 3·4, 3·4.'

I can beat that, Roz thought.

Her throat was dry, and she fancied that everyone could hear the thudding of her heart as she took her position. One ... two ... three ... four. Music flooded the rink and she plunged into the complex routine of spins and jumps that her coach had choreographed to the music of *Carousel*. The fast section ended with a double axel and as she landed she heard a burst of applause. Then she glided into a spin as the music changed to the slow sadness of *You'll Never Walk Alone*. Just listening to it gave her a lump in the throat, and the choreography, with its long, graceful arm movements and slow arabesques, mirrored her feelings.

Then she was into the last minute of the routine. The bouncy rhythm of the Clambake number jerked the audience into a fever of clapping in time to the music. They were so noisy that she nearly lost the last few bars, but somehow managed to catch the rhythm again just in time to dig in the left toe pick behind her, and fling her arms up on the very last note.

It was great. The best she'd ever done. Shaking with relief she skated across to the judges and curtsied, before going back to the barrier.

'For Technical Merit, 3·7, 3·8, 3·8, 3·8.'

Brilliant. She wiped her neck with the towel, taking in great gulps of air. Then came the next set of marks.

'Artistic Impression, 3·8, 3·9, 3·9, 3·8.'

She heard a burst of applause, and was suddenly conscious of her form in the front row. They were still clapping her performance as Louise skated on to the ice to start her routine.

It wasn't a bad performance. She landed on two feet instead of one on her first jump, but other than that not bad at all. But she seemed to have lost the will to win. It was as if she were on automatic pilot. As if she had given up before she had really started. And the marks reflected that. One 3·5. That was the highest mark she got.

The last girl in the section was hopeless. She slipped and fell halfway through her routine and went to pieces after that. No contest there. Roz was the clear winner, and as she went up to receive her medal, she saw her mother smiling proudly from the crowd.

In the break, the Polar Bear Ice machine lumbered on to the ice to get it ready for the show-skating exhibition that was to follow. Roz saw Sula weaving her way through the skaters towards her. 'That was fantastic!' she gasped. 'I never thought you were that good. Miss Jenkyns is really stunned. Come and talk.'

'I can't. I've got to get changed. We're doing a circus scene, and Tony and I are the clowns.'

'Is that your brother?' Sula asked, gazing past her towards the seats where her mother and Tony were sitting.

'Yeah.'

'He doesn't look a bit like you. You're so dark.'

'I follow my mum. She's from Russia.'

Sula blinked. 'You're a cool one, Ratty. You never tell me anything.'

Roz grinned. 'Well I am telling you now. Anyway, I must go and change.'

With ginger wigs and comic makeup, Tony and Roz were waiting behind the barrier at the far end of the rinks as the lights dimmed for the circus scene.

Roz's nervousness had completely disappeared. This would be fun, she thought. They had worked on the routine so often she could do it with her eyes shut. She studied the audience carefully. Yes, it couldn't have been better. Miss Jenkyns and the rest of the class would have a real eyeful.

The brassy overture faded, and the DJ's voice crackled out over the microphone. 'Our first number in this section of the programme is, "Entry of the Clowns", with Tony and Rosanne Tompkin. The mums and dads in the audience will perhaps remember Rosanne Andrianov – the champion Russian skater who took the gold medal three years running in the 1970s? Well, Tony and Roz are her children, so a big welcome please to . . . *Tony and Rosanne Tompkin.*'

It was a crazy routine – simple but effective – in which they soaked each other with bucket after bucket of water. Every so often one would stagger towards the audience as if they were going to pour the water over them, then skilfully spin round so that the water dashed harmlessly on to the ice.

The music was coming to a climax. Roz skated across to the barrier to refill her bucket – only this time from the other container.

She zig-zagged jerkily towards where the class were sitting, acting as if the bucket was so heavy that it would trip her up at any moment. Sula and the others were laughing and giggling like crazy, and even Miss Jenkyns and Louise, who were sitting at the end of the row. Roz paused, then spun round to face them, swinging the bucket in time to the music.

'Shall I?' she asked the audience.

'Yes!' The answer came back in a roar.

'One . . .'

'Two,' they yelled delightedly.

'*Three!*' In one swift movement she tossed the contents of the bucket towards them, then went skating away behind the curtains at the far end of the barrier.

Louise screamed hysterically. She hardly seemed to notice that the frothy white torrent that shot from the bucket was not the ice-cold water that they had been expecting – but a flurry of feathers. And even when she did, she just sat there open mouthed . . . one curly white feather quivering gently on her upper lip.

The rest of the form went wild. 'Serves you right,' someone shouted. Then they all began to chant . . .

'Ratty. Ratty. We want Ratty!' The rest of the audience took it up. 'Ratty. Ratty. We want Ratty.'

Roz and her brother skated out into the spotlight to take their bow. She glanced towards the row where her form were sitting, and her eyes widened with surprise. Louise had disappeared, but Miss Jenkyns was still there – brushing off the feathers and chanting with the rest.

'Ratty. Ratty. We want Ratty.' Not Rosanne. Or even Roz. But Ratty. And everyone was smiling. As if they really liked her.

Roz grinned. Suddenly the hated nickname didn't seem so bad after all.

You're Late, Dad

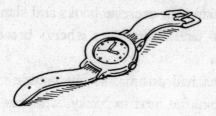

TONY BRADMAN

Steven's classroom was at the front of the school, and his desk was next to the window. So, just by turning his head slightly, he could see most of the street outside.

It was almost lunchtime, and they were supposed to be doing silent reading, but Steven couldn't concentrate on his book, even though it was a good one. He couldn't stop thinking about the afternoon. It was Sports Day and he knew, he just *knew* that he was going to win a race. And Dad had promised to be there.

Steven looked up. Mr Brooks was marking a huge pile of exercise books with a frown on his face. It was very quiet. All Steven could hear was the sound of Mr Brooks picking up exercise books and slapping them down again, and Samantha's wheezy breathing close behind him.

Samantha had asthma, so she couldn't be in any races. But she sat next to Nicky, who was the fastest runner in the school, or so everyone said. He *was* fast, but Steven knew he was going to beat him today. He could see the end of the race in his mind, in slow motion, just the way it was on the TV. He'd burst through the tape, Nicky miles behind him, and Dad would be right there, cheering him on. It was going to be great. No it wasn't . . . it was going to be amazing!

Out of the corner of his eye, Steven saw something moving in the street. He turned quickly, but carefully, so no one would notice, and saw a car stop. But it was a red Metro, not Dad's dark blue Ford. It was too early for him to arrive yet, anyway. Sports Day didn't start till two o'clock.

Steven just hoped he wasn't going to be late this time.

Steven's dad looked at his watch and swore under his breath. It was nearly twelve . . . where had the morning gone? He'd got nothing done, even though he'd been frantically busy from the moment he'd sat down at his desk. The phone hadn't stopped ringing, so he hadn't even made a start on that report. And it was supposed to be finished today.

He did some quick mental arithmetic. If he started it now, right now, he could probably finish it in an hour or so. It would take him five minutes to get to the car park, then half an hour to get to the school. He smiled to himself. There was plenty of time.

He pulled a pad towards him from the mess of papers on his desk, picked up his pen, and thought. A sentence began to form itself in his mind, but evaporated when the phone rang.

'Hello, Jim Morris speaking,' he said.

'Hello, Jim, Bob Daniels here.'

Jim sat up straight in his chair. Bob Daniels was his boss, and a very important man.

'Could you come over to my office for a meeting this afternoon, Jim? About three o'clock?'

Jim explained that he had already asked for the afternoon off to go to his son's Sports Day.

'Oh yes, I remember now . . .' said Bob Daniels. He paused. 'That's a bit of a nuisance, Jim.'

Jim knew the boss wasn't pleased about it. Bob Daniels liked his employees to do what *he* wanted, and

29

show him what wonderful workers they were. He didn't think they should have time off for things like Sports Days.

'Can't your wife go instead?' he was saying. 'This *is* very important.'

'That's impossible, I'm afraid,' said Jim curtly. He was cross now . . . Bob Daniels knew he was divorced.

'Well, pop in and see me before you go. I'd like a chat . . .'

Jim said he would, and put the phone down. He looked at his watch, then started writing very fast.

Steven picked at his food. He was too excited to eat, and besides, he didn't really like macaroni cheese. He pushed his plate away.

'Are you leaving all that?' said Nicky, who was sitting opposite him. 'I'll have it if you don't want it.'

Steven said OK, and soon Nicky was scooping leftovers into his mouth as fast as he could go. Steven tried to concentrate on his yoghurt, but his eyes kept drifting back to the lumps of macaroni cheese disappearing into Nicky.

'Is your mum coming this afternoon?' Nicky said between mouthfuls. He didn't wait for an answer. 'Mine is, and my dad said he'd be there too . . .'

Steven let Nicky's voice wash over him. Nicky's

mum and dad would definitely be there, with his little brother, his baby sister, his granny and grandpa, an aunt or two, and even the dog, probably. His entire family always seemed to come to everything at the school, whatever it was, whenever it happened.

Steven's mum came to the school sometimes. She'd managed to get the afternoon off from her job for the Harvest Festival, and for the Christmas Concert. And when the headmistress had written to her about his school work, and how he needed to pull up his socks, she had come in to see her the very next morning.

But Steven's dad hadn't been to the school for years, not since before the divorce.

At first his mum wouldn't let him see Steven at all. Then they'd come to an agreement, and Dad was allowed to take him out on a Saturday. He was supposed to arrive at ten-thirty and bring Steven back at one o'clock. But he was always late. Most Saturdays Steven spent ages standing at the window . . . waiting.

It hadn't mattered so much at first. Then Steven's mum got the job in the shop and had to work on Saturday mornings. Dad was supposed to pick Steven up at nine-thirty now. She got really angry when he was late, as he was every week, without fail.

Last Saturday they had stood arguing in the street with Steven standing between them. He had closed his eyes and remembered all the nights he'd spent lying in bed, listening to his parents shout and fight downstairs.

He didn't miss all that. But he did miss Dad, although he never told Mum how he felt. She didn't like talking about Dad or the divorce, and Steven didn't want to upset her. They got on OK most of the time, and underneath it all she was still the same old Mum. But she was always so busy these days, and when she wasn't busy she was tired. And she hardly ever smiled.

Dad didn't do much smiling either. He lived in a poky little flat on the other side of town, and Steven knew he hated taking him there on a Saturday. That was why they spent most of their time together in the park, or at McDonalds, or driving out into the country to see the sights they'd seen a million times before.

When his mum told Dad how difficult it was to get an afternoon off for Sports Day, Steven's heart had sunk. There would be no one there to cheer him on. And then Dad had said *he* would come. Steven had been amazed – and really, really pleased.

'I'll believe it when I see it,' his mum had said as she'd marched off down the street to work. But his dad had promised.

'Don't you worry, son,' he'd said. 'I'll be there.'

Nicky was eating an apple now, and still talking. Steven looked beyond him at the clock on the wall. It was one-twenty. He wondered where his dad was, right at that moment.

The lift wasn't working, so Jim ran down the stairs as fast as he could. By the time he got to the bottom, seven floors below his office, he was taking them three at a time. He swung round the bannister at the end, and ran towards the main doors, nearly knocking the security man over as he shot out.

He was right in the middle of the shopping centre. Today it seemed as if everyone within one hundred miles had come in to shop. Jim could hardly get through the crowds. It usually only took him five minutes to reach the car park, but at this rate he'd be lucky if he ever got there at all.

He tried to run, dodging past the old-age pensioners, the mums with pushchairs, bumping into people and shouting sorry over his shoulder. It was a warm day, and soon he could feel the sweat dripping off his forehead. His shirt stuck to his back, and his suit jacket felt as if it weighed a ton.

It was Bob Daniels' fault that he was late. Jim had gone to see him on his way out, and had been treated to a little lecture about how his work had been suffering, how he needed to pull up his socks if he wanted to get on . . . All he'd wanted to do by then was to get out, but you can't really hurry your boss when he's giving you a telling off. He'd just let the words wash over him in the end. He knew he wasn't doing his best at work, and he worried about it. Money had been really tight since the divorce, and it was getting harder just to make ends meet. The last thing he needed was to lose his job.

Barbara was right though; it wasn't fair that she should be the one to go to Steven's school all the time. But she didn't seem to realise how difficult it was to explain things to a boss like Bob Daniels. It always ended in a row when they talked about it, and Steven hated them rowing. Sometimes he felt as if he was hardly part of Steven's life any more, but he didn't know what to do about it. Nothing was easy now. Everything was a mess.

Jim ran into the car park. His car was on the fifth floor, but the lift there wasn't working either, so he turned to go up the dark, dirty, graffiti-covered stairway. He stopped to get his breath back, and looked at his watch. It was one thirty-three. He had a sudden vision of his son's face wearing a look of complete disappointment.

'I'll make it, Steven,' he said aloud as he ran up the first flight. 'I *swear* I'll make it.'

'I don't think your dad's going to make it,' said Nicky. Steven didn't say anything. He just kept his eyes fixed on the street beyond the fence around the school playing fields. He wasn't sure, but he thought his dad would have to come that way when he finally arrived. If he ever got there.

'He'll make it,' he said.

'You can always come and stand with us while you wait,' said Nicky. He waved in the direction of his family, a large group of people standing nearby. There were lots of small children with them, as well as several dogs, and they were all laughing and making a lot of noise. Steven didn't reply.

'Suit yourself,' said Nicky. He walked off, and Steven watched him go. He wished now that he hadn't said anything about his dad coming, but it had all spilled out while they were getting changed. Nicky had been going on about his dad, and how he'd been a really great runner when he was at school.

'My dad was a good runner too,' Steven had said. And before he could stop himself, he was saying all sorts of things about his dad that weren't true, about how he'd been a brilliant runner and won loads of

35

cups and medals. Nicky had looked as if he didn't believe him, which only made Steven say even more.

But now it was nearly two o'clock, and there was no sign of Dad anywhere. He was going to be late, that was for sure, but Steven had half expected that. It wouldn't matter so long as he got there before the big race, the four hundred metres, and that wasn't until two-thirty. So there was still time.

'Starters for the first race please!' Mr Brooks called out. A gaggle of children surrounded him. 'Not all at once, not all at once,' he shouted crossly, and began handing out coloured bibs with numbers on.

Steven looked towards the street again.

'Come on, Dad,' he whispered. 'Where *are* you?'

Jim drummed his fingers on the steering wheel. The car in front hadn't moved for the last five minutes, and as far ahead as he could see there was a long line of cars, all well and truly stuck in a traffic jam.

He just couldn't believe it. It had taken him nearly ten minutes to get out of the car park, and another ten to get on to the bypass. Now here he was on what was supposed to be the fast route – and he wasn't moving at all.

He should have cut across town . . . it couldn't have been any slower. He daren't look at his watch. He knew he was late and he didn't want to know *how* late any more.

Suddenly the car in front started moving, and soon the line of cars was edging slowly along. Jim sat up in his seat and tried to see what was happening. Four or five cars ahead the line was slowing to a stop again. But just then, he saw an 'Exit' sign coming up on his left.

'Right,' he said aloud. He sat back in his seat, swung the steering wheel over hard, and hit the accelerator. He shot away with a squeal of tyres, raced into the exit slip road and headed for town.

'Nothing's going to beat me today,' he whispered as the engine roared. He was determined to make it. 'Nothing . . .'

'Right,' said Mr Brooks. 'Starters for the four hundred metres, fourth-year boys. Come on, we haven't got all day!'

Steven and the others in the race took their numbered bibs from him. There were eight of them altogether, and Steven was number three, Nicky number two. So they'd be next to each other.

'Line up now,' Mr Brooks was saying. Steven found his lane, and stood while the others found theirs.

'Come on, Nicky!' someone called from the crowd at the side of the track. Other voices joined in. 'You can do it, Nicky! You can do it!' Nicky smiled and waved, then clasped his hands and raised them over his head like a champion.

Steven looked away, towards the street. There was no sign of a dark blue Ford, no sign of his dad. He wasn't going to make it. He wouldn't be there. He'd broken his promise.

'To your marks please, boys,' Mr Brooks said. The eight boys were now in their lanes, poised, waiting for the start. Steven looked down at the toe of his trainer on the white line just in front of him. He could hear a buzz of voices, then everything seemed to go quiet. His throat felt tight, and his eyes were prickling.

A tear ran down his cheek and fell on a white-painted blade of grass. It made the white run.

'Ready . . . steady . . .'

There was a bang, and Steven was running.

Jim swung the car round the corner and squealed to a halt in the first space he could see. One of the front wheels hit the curb with a clunk, and he knew without looking that the back of the car was sticking well out into the road. But he didn't care.

He flung open the door, jumped out and started

running past the school fence. He could hear a crowd cheering and calling names, and as he looked he could see some children running round the track on the playing fields.

He came to the school gates at last, and ran through. He didn't stop, but ran straight on, past the main building, past the playground, past the infants sitting in a group with their teachers, past the headmistress and the head of the board of governors, who both stared at him open-mouthed, and right up to the winning line . . .

. . . Just as two boys came off the last bend and headed for the tape. They were neck and neck, each straining to get in front of the other.

Steven could feel Nicky right next to him. He could hear voices calling Nicky's name, he could feel his legs getting tired, his heart beating as if it was going to explode, his lungs bursting. He wasn't going to make it.

'Come on, Steven!' Someone was calling out *his* name. 'Come on, Steven, you can do it!'

There wasn't far to go now. Steven could see the tape, and standing beyond it he could see his dad. He ran, he ran as fast as he could. He burst through the tape and into his dad's arms.

At first neither of them could speak. They were both out of breath, puffing and panting and holding on to each other. Out of the corner of his eye, Steven could see Nicky's mum and dad walking off with him, their arms round his shoulders. Nicky looked back at him, but Steven didn't care about anything or anyone else.

He freed a hand to wipe his eyes, then stepped back and looked up at his dad.

'Steven, I . . .' Jim started to say.

'You're late, Dad,' said Steven, but he smiled as he said it. His dad smiled back, then put an arm round Steven's shoulder. They walked off together towards the others.

The Twelve Labours
of Heracles*

RETOLD BY
GERALDINE MCCAUGHREAN

There was once a baby born who was so remarkable
that the gods themselves stared down at his cradle. He
was called Heracles, and when huge snakes slithered
into his crib to strangle him, he knotted and plaited
them as if they were pieces of string, and threw them
out again.

For Heracles was strong – fantastically strong –
stronger than you and me and a hundred others put

---

*Heracles is the Greek name for Hercules

together. Fortunately, he was also gentle and kind, so that his friends had nothing to fear from him. His schoolteacher made him promise never to touch alcoholic drink though. 'If you were ever to get drunk, Heracles,' the schoolmaster said, 'who knows what terrible thing you might do with that great strength of yours!'

Heracles promised, and he truly meant to keep his promise. But then his friends all drank at parties, his family always had wine with their meals: it seemed foolish for Heracles to ask for fruit juice or water. So he was tempted to take just one glass of wine – and after that another – and another – and another. Soon he was roaring drunk, throwing punches in all directions. When the wine's work was done, Heracles's own family lay dead on the floor, and Heracles was an outcast hated by everyone and most of all by himself.

For his crime, he was condemned to serve King Eurystheus as a slave for seven years. Eurystheus was a mean, spiteful man, whose kingdom was overrun by a great many problems, and he decided to set Heracles the twelve most dangerous tasks he could think of – tasks that were to become known as the Twelve Labours of Heracles.

A giant lion was terrorizing his kingdom, eating

men, women and children. 'Go and kill the lion, slave,' he told Heracles.

Heracles was so miserable that he did not much care whether he lived or died. He found the lion's den and strode in, with no weapon but his bare hands. When the beast sprang at him, Heracles took it by the throat and shook it like a rug, then wrung it out like washing. When it was dead, he skinned it and wore the lion skin for a tunic, knotting the paws around his waist and shoulders.

If King Eurystheus was grateful, he did not show it, but simply set Heracles his Second Labour. 'If you can kill lions,' he said, 'you may as well try to kill the Hydra.'

The Hydra was a water serpent which lived in the middle of a swamp. When it was born it had nine heads, but each time one was cut off, two new heads grew to replace it. By the time Heracles came face to face with the Hydra, it had fifty heads, all gnashing their horrible teeth.

Heracles was quick with his sword and nimble on his feet. But though he slashed through many snaking necks without being bitten, the struggle only became more difficult. The heads just multiplied! So Heracles ran off a short way and lit a fire. Then he heated his wooden club red-hot and, with his sword in one hand and his club in the other, he re-entered the fight.

This time, as he cut through each neck, he singed the ragged end with his red-hot club, and the head did not regrow. At last the Hydra looked like nothing more than a knobbly tree stump.

There was no time to rest after fighting the Hydra. King Eurystheus sent him to capture a stag with golden antlers, then to kill a huge wild boar.

Heracles's Fifth Labour was a particularly unpleasant one: to clean the Augean stables.

Lord Augeas kept one thousand animals penned up in sties and stables stretching the length of a foul valley. He was too idle to clean out his animals and too mean to hire farmhands. So the wretched beasts stood up to their bellies in dung. People for miles around complained about the smell.

Heracles stood on a hilltop, looking down on the valley, holding his nose. He saw a river bubbling close by, and it gave him an idea. Moving boulders as easily as if they were feather pillows, he built a dam so that the river flowed out of its course and down the valley instead. Startled horses and cows and goats and sheep staggered in a torrent of rushing water, but the dung beneath them was scoured away by the river. Heracles only had to demolish the dam with one blow of his club, and the river flowed back to its old river bed.

The animals stood shivering and shaking themselves dry in a green, clean valley.

King Eurystheus was ready and waiting with his next three commands. Heracles was to destroy a flock of bloodthirsty man-eating birds, tame the mad bull of Crete, and capture the famous wild horses which could run faster than the wind.

By now the king had begun to feel very nervous of his slave. He had a big bronze vase made and hid inside it whenever Heracles came back from doing his work.

'The mad bull is tamed, master. The man-eating birds are dead, and your wild horses are outside in the yard,' said Heracles, when he returned soon after. 'What must I do next?'

But Eurystheus was running out of problems and his mind turned to thoughts of getting rich with the help of Heracles.

'Get me the jewelled belt worn by the Queen of the Amazons!' said the king from inside his urn.

Here was one task for which Heracles did not mean to use his great strength. He simply went to the queen of those savage female warriors and explained why he was there. She took an instant liking to him and gave him the belt straight away. Unfortunately, word spread through the camp that Heracles had come to kill the queen and he had to fight a thousand angry women, fierce as wasps, before he could escape with the jewelled belt.

And so it continued. No sooner did Heracles finish one task, than he was set another one. To fetch King Eurystheus the legendary giant oxen, Heracles made a bridge over the sea by bending two mountain peaks out across the water. To fetch Pluto's three-headed dog, Cerberus, he travelled down to the fearful Underworld.

But the twelfth and last and greediest of the king's commands was for Heracles to bring him the apples of the Hesperides. These magical fruit grew on a tree in a garden at the end of the world, and around that tree coiled a dragon which never slept.

Even Heracles, with all his courage and strength, quailed at the thought of fighting the dragon. Better by far that a friend should ask it for the fruit and be allowed to take them. So Heracles went to see a giant named Atlas.

Now Atlas was no ordinary giant, as big as a house. Atlas was the biggest man in the world, and towered above houses, trees, cliffs and hills. He was so tall that the gods had given him the task of holding up the sky and keeping the stars from falling. The sun scorched his neck and the new moon shaved his beard. And for thousands of years he had stood in the one spot.

'How can I go to the end of the world?' said Atlas, when Heracles asked him for the favour. 'How can I go *anywhere*?'

'I could hold the sky for you while you were gone,' suggested Heracles.

'Could you? Would you? Then I'll do it!' said Atlas.

So Heracles took the sky on his back – though it was the heaviest burden he had ever carried. Atlas stretched himself, then strode away towards the end of the world: the gardeners were members of his family.

Fetching the apples was no hardship. But as the giant hurried back across the world, carrying the precious fruit, he thought how wonderful it felt to be free! As he got closer to home, the thought of carrying that weight of sky again seemed less and less attractive. His steps slowed. When at last he reached Heracles – poor exhausted, bone-bent Heracles – Atlas exclaimed, 'I've decided! I'm going to let *you* go on holding up the sky, and I'll deliver these apples to King Eurystheus.'

There was a silence. Then Heracles grunted, 'Fine. Thank you. It's a great honour to be allowed to hold up heaven. But if you could just help me get a pad across my shoulders before you go . . . these stars do prickle . . .'

So Atlas took charge of the sky again – just while Heracles made a pad for his shoulders. He even gave Heracles the apples to hold, because he needed both hands.

'Well, I'll be on my way now,' said Heracles, juggling with the apples as he scurried away. 'Most grateful for your help. Perhaps next time, *you*'ll get the better of *me*.'

After seven years, Heracles's hard labours came to an end, and he was free. But he was never free from his sorrow at taking that first glass of wine: not until the day he died.

Being only a man and not a god, he did die. But the gods did not forget him. They cut him out in stars and hung him in the sky, to rest from his labours for all time, among the singing planets.

Helping Hercules

FRANCESCA SIMON

Susan was not what you would call helpful. Her parents nagged her to do more tidying, but it did no good. In Susan's opinion, parents should do all the housework, leaving children free to enjoy thselves. She had far better things to do with *her* time than hoover the sitting-room or dust the shelves.

Her parents, unfortunately, did not agree.

Every Sunday night her father handed out the weekly chores.

'Fred, you empty the wastepaper baskets,' said Dad. (When Susan did it she made sure most of the rubbish ended up on the carpet.)

'OK,' said Fred, who was only five and got all the easy tasks.

'Eileen, you set and clear the table,' said Dad. (When Susan did it she broke at least one plate and wiped all the crumbs straight on to the floor.)

'Sure,' said Eileen.

'Susan, you can clean out the kitten litter tray,' said Dad.

'It's not fair! I always get the worst jobs!' howled Susan.

'I cleaned the kitty litter last week,' said Eileen. 'Now it's your turn.'

'Everyone in this family has to help out,' said Dad.

'I'm far too busy and I'm not your slave,' snarled Susan. 'Clean it out yourself.' She didn't even like the cat. Stinky's main pleasure in life was throwing up on the stairs and leaping on to laps with his claws out.

'SUSAN!' said Dad.

'I won't do it!' shrieked Susan. 'I hate this!'

'Go to your room,' said Dad. 'And don't come down until you're ready to help.'

Susan flounced upstairs and went into her bedroom, giving the door a good loud slam. Just in case the task-masters downstairs hadn't heard, she opened her door and banged it shut again a few more times.

She'd show them. She'd starve before she came

down and then they'd be sorry. She'd have a great time right here.

Susan looked around her messy room. She could play with her knights but she wasn't really in the mood, especially since that brat Fred had snapped off all the horses' tails. She could practise her recorder . . . no way. Her bossy parents liked hearing her play.

Then Susan saw the old cigar box tucked up on a high shelf. Aha! Her coin collection. She hadn't looked at it for ages, and she had that new Greek coin Uncle Martin had given her for her birthday.

Susan kicked her way through the dirty clothes, books and papers littering the floor, pulled her collection down from the shelf – knocking off a stack of books in the process – and got out her coin catalogue.

Then she unwrapped the precious coin. It had belonged to her grandfather and great-grandfather before him, Uncle Martin had said. Now it was hers. Susan took the silver coin in her hands, and looked at it carefully.

The coin was small and round, with worn, uneven edges. The front showed a man wearing a lion-skin cloak and holding a ferocious boar. Well, that was easy enough, it was Hercules. She flipped it over. But instead of the head of a god or goddess, there were strange signs and carvings.

51

Susan opened her catalogue, and searched. She looked at every picture of the Ancient Greek coins and then looked again. Then she checked the Roman coins to see if it could be there, even though she knew perfectly well it was Greek. But there was no sign of this coin.

How odd. There were two possibilities here. One, that the coin was so rare – and so valuable – that it was not in her catalogue. The second possibility – no. That was too silly for words.

Susan sat on her bed and held the coin up to the light. Was her mind playing tricks, or did a strange, dull gleam come from Hercules's eyes? She turned the coin over in her fingers, feeling its scratched, worn surface. Was it her imagination, or did the coin feel a little bit warm?

Naturally, Susan did not believe in magic. Only little kids like Fred believed in nonsense like flying carpets, magic lamps, and wishing wells.

'OK coin, if you're magic, I wish . . .' Susan paused for a moment and closed her eyes, 'I wish that I could fly around the room.' She opened her eyes. She was still plonked on her bed.

'Ha,' said Susan, feeling a bit silly.

'I wish,' said Susan, 'that everything on the floor would put itself away.'

She opened her eyes. Her bedroom was as big a pigsty as ever.

How silly I am, thought Susan. Then she looked at the coin and smiled.

'I wish,' said Susan, closing her eyes and rubbing the coin between her fingers, 'that I could meet Hercules.'

Next moment, the bed seemed to give way and she fell heavily to the ground. But instead of falling on the familiar grey carpet, she landed on a cold stone floor.

Susan blinked. Her bedroom was gone. She was in the corner of an immense room, with stone columns, walls black with smoke, embroidered hangings and flickering torches. Men lined the walls on either side, all standing to attention, their eyes fixed on a little man huddled against the back of a large throne.

In front of her towered a giant man wearing a yellow lion-skin tied over his shoulder and round his waist. The lion's fanged head glowered on top of his, like a bristling helmet. A great sword dangled by his side, and a quiver full of arrows hung from his shoulders. A huge olive-wood club lay beside him. In his arms the man held up a bellowing boar.

I must be dreaming, thought Susan.

Then the giant flung the frantic beast on to the floor. Its tied feet lashed the ground.

'Here's the Erymanthian boar, Eurystheus!' boomed Hercules, for of course it was he.

The little man leaped out of his throne and started howling.

'Get that thing out of here!' shrieked Eurystheus. Then he scrambled into a large brass pot, screaming with terror, 'OUT! OUT! OUT!'

The giant laughed, scooped up the writhing boar as if it were a bag of sugar, walked up to the open double doors and hurled the snorting boar through them. A few moments later, Susan heard a gigantic splash.

I haven't got my wish, this is only a dream, thought Susan. No need to worry.

But just in case she crept behind an urn.

Hercules stomped back into the room.

'Is that boar gone yet?' whimpered the voice from the brass pot.

'It's gone, you big coward,' sneered Hercules. 'I flung it into the sea. I'll bet it's halfway to Crete by now.'

Two fingers appeared on top of the jar.

'Are you sure?' whined the king.

'YES,' snarled Hercules.

'Don't you ever bring any more wild animals to my palace again,' said Eurystheus, climbing back on to his throne. He smoothed his rumpled tunic and took hold again of his sceptre. The men lining the walls leaned forward, awaiting orders.

'Right, Hercules, next labour,' said the king, and he started to giggle. 'It's the smelliest, stinkiest, most horrible job in the whole world and you'll never ever be able to do it! Killing the lion and the hydra and capturing the hind with the golden horns and that boar was nothing compared to this! You've heard of King Augeas at Elis and his three thousand cattle? Well, I order you to go and clean out his stables in one day. And better bring something to plug your nose – those stables haven't been cleaned for thirty years – ha ha ha!'

Hercules scowled but said nothing.

'Who's this?' said the king suddenly, pointing straight at Susan.

I'm out of here, thought Susan. She rubbed the coin, which she still had clutched in her hand, and wished frantically to be home.

Nothing happened.

Then strong arms grabbed her and pushed her before Eurystheus.

'Who are you?' demanded the king.

'I'm Susan,' said Susan, trying to stop her voice from shaking.

'Where are you from?'

'London,' said Susan.

'Never heard of it,' said the king. He looked at her more closely, and a big smile spread across his face.

'See this girl, Hercules?' said the king. 'You take her along to clean the stables. I'm sure she'll be a great help.'

'What!' screamed Hercules.

'And mind you keep her alive – that's part of your labour too,' said the king, rubbing his hands.

Hercules glared at Susan. She glared back at him. But before she could say anything he tucked her under his arm, strode out of the palace and started walking along the cliffs high above the choppy, wine-dark sea.

'Put me down!' ordered Susan. 'Put me down!'

Hercules ignored her.

'I can walk by myself, thank you very much,' said Susan.

'Listen, pipsqueak,' snapped Hercules. 'I don't like this any more than you do. But the sooner we get to King Augeas at Elis and muck out his filthy cattle the sooner you and I can go our separate ways.'

'I'm not helping you,' said Susan. 'I'm not your slave. Clean out your own stables.'

'Do you realize, brat, that I could crush you with my little toe?' snapped Hercules.

'You have to keep me alive – the king said so,' said Susan.

Hercules gnashed his teeth.

'I'm bigger than you, and you'll do what I say,' he growled.

'Bully!' said Susan.

Hercules twisted his thick neck and stared at her.

'Watch your tongue, you little worm,' said Hercules. 'I'm famous for my bad temper.'

'So am I,' said Susan.

'Oh yeah?' said Hercules.

'Yeah,' said Susan. 'When my sister Eileen squirted me with a water pistol I hit her. So go on, what's the worst thing you ever did?'

'When I was a boy my music teacher slapped me for playing a wrong note so I whacked him with my lyre and killed him,' said Hercules.

Susan gasped. That was pretty terrible. She didn't think hitting Eileen was quite on the same level.

'What a grump you are, Hercules,' said Susan.

Hercules gripped his great olive-wood club.

'You'd be grumpy too if you were a slave to a snotty little toe-rag like Eurystheus and had to do whatever horrible job he set you.'

'Humph,' said Susan. 'So when do we get to the stables?'

'Soon,' said Hercules.

'How soon is soon?' said Susan. 'I have better things to do with my time than help *you*.'

'Be quiet,' said Hercules. 'And stop whining.'

On and on and on they travelled.

'Aren't we there yet?' moaned Susan for the hundredth time. Then she sniffed. The fresh smell of olive groves had suddenly changed into something less pleasant.

Hercules sniffed.

'Yup,' he said. 'We're getting near King Augeas's stables.'

A few more strides and the stink was overwhelming.

'Pooh,' said Susan. 'What a smell.'

'Pretty bad,' said Hercules grimly.

They walked in silence through the choking stench until they stood in the stable yard. Far off in the distance Susan could see thousands of cattle grazing in the fields between two rivers.

Susan stared at the huge stables. Never in her most horrible nightmares had she ever seen so much filth and dung. The sludgy, slimy, stinky mucky piles went on for miles.

And the smell – goodness gracious, it was awful!

Hercules looked glum.

'Right, to work,' he said.

'What's your plan?' asked Susan.

'Get that bucket and start shovelling. We'll heap all the muck out here.'

Susan gaped at him.

'*That's* your plan?' she said. 'We'll never finish in a day.'

'Shut up and start mucking out,' ordered Hercules.

Very, very reluctantly, Susan got her bucket. Even more reluctantly, she picked up a shovel. Holding her nose with one hand, she approached the first reeking corner. Of all the magic adventures in the world, she got to clean out a stable.

'Yuck!' squealed Susan. She poked her shovel gingerly into the nearest cattle dung.

'Bleech!' She tossed the first noxious shovelful into the stable yard.

'Pooh! Ugh! Gross!' This was worse than cleaning out the kitty litter. This was a million billion trillion times worse than cleaning out the kitty litter. If she ever got back home she would never complain again.

Beside her, Hercules shovelled like a whirlwind, bending and hurling and twisting so fast she could hardly see him.

Half an hour passed.

'Right, ten stalls down, only 2,870 to go,' said Hercules.

'Actually 2,990,' corrected Susan. 'At this rate, we'll be here five years. You're supposed to clean these stables in a day.'

'Just keep working,' snapped Hercules, digging ferociously. 'If you're so smart you come up with a better plan.'

Susan scowled. She could not bear the stench another second.

'Wait a minute,' said Susan. An idea had flashed into her head. She looked at Hercules.

'Just how strong are you?' she said.

Hercules went up to the thick stone wall at the side of the stable building and punched a gaping hole into it with one swing of his club.

'THAT STRONG!' bellowed Hercules.

'Then listen,' said Susan. 'I've got a great idea. Remember those rivers we crossed coming here?'

'The Alpheus and the Peneus? So?'

'What if you dug a channel and diverted the rivers to run through the stables,' said Susan. 'The current would do the work for us and wash away all this muck. All you'd have to do is knock holes in the stable walls at either end, and then rebuild them once the stables were clean. Oh yes, and turn the rivers back to their original beds.'

Hercules stared at her.

'Hmmm,' he said. 'Hmmm,' he said again.

Then he grabbed his club and ran off.

Soon Susan heard a shout.

'Watch out! Water's coming!'

Susan dashed into the fields, just in time to see a torrent of water pour into the stables.

In no time at all they were washed clean.

Susan cheered as she watched Hercules rebuild the walls and force the rivers back to their beds.

'That's that,' said Hercules, looking over the sparkling stables with satisfaction. 'Time for me to head back to that snivelling slave-driver. You're free to go, so bye bye.'

Go where, thought Susan frantically. She fumbled in her pocket and took out the coin.

'Wait. Look at this,' she said, handing it to Hercules.

He took the coin and gazed at it. Slowly he turned it over and over.

'It's me,' he said at last. 'I'm famous. Of course my muscles are much bigger than this picture shows but it's not bad. Don't I look handsome?'

'You look OK,' said Susan. 'Turn it over. What does that writing say?'

Hercules looked for a long time at the Greek letters. Had he killed his Greek teacher too, Susan wondered, before he'd learned to read?

'It says, TI ETHELEIS – What do you wish?' he said at last.

'I wish to go home,' said Susan.

'So go,' said Hercules.

'I can't,' said Susan. 'I don't know how. I wished that before and it didn't happen.'

'That's how these magic things work,' said Hercules. 'You never quite know why or how. Let me try it. I wish a fountain would burst out of the ground when I stamp my foot.'

He stamped. The earth trembled, but no water appeared.

'See,' said Susan sadly. 'It's not very reliable. Can I have it back please?'

'Sorry,' said Hercules, grinning stupidly at his carved picture. 'I'm keeping this.'

'Give me back my coin!' shouted Susan.

'No,' said Hercules. 'Finders keepers.'

'You didn't find it! I just showed it to you!' she screamed.

'Tough,' said Hercules.

Susan scowled at him.

'I need that coin to get home,' she said. 'Is this the

62

thanks I get? Or do you want people to know that the great Hercules needed a girl's help to complete one of his labours?'

Hercules paused.

'All right,' he said. 'I'll give the coin back if you swear on oath you will keep your part in my labour a secret.'

'I swear,' said Susan.

'Swear by the river Styx, the black river of Hades,' said Hercules.

'I swear by the river Styx,' said Susan.

Hercules took one last look at his picture, then reluctantly gave her back the coin. Susan rubbed it between her fingers and wished.

At once she felt herself falling. But instead of landing in the dirt she found herself stretched out on her own soft bed.

Susan rubbed her head. She felt dizzy.

'Gosh, what a horrible dream,' said Susan, looking at the coin clasped tightly in her fist. Then she went to her bookshelf, took down her book of Greek myths and quickly read through Hercules's labours.

'What a creep!' she said. 'He *did* take all the credit for cleaning the stables. I suppose that's not surprising. Hold on, I'm being silly,' she said, thumping herself. 'It was only a dream.'

She ran out of her bedroom.

'Mum, Dad, I'm ready to help now!' she shouted, clambering down the stairs. She paused at the kitchen door, where her family were eating dinner.

Everyone stared at her.

'What's wrong?' said Susan.

Eileen choked.

Stinky stalked out of the room.

Fred held his nose.

'Pooh,' he said, waving his hand in front of his face.

'Where have you been?' said Dad. 'You smell like you've been living in a stable.'

Leaf Magic

MARGARET MAHY

When Michael ran home from school, he heard the wind at his heels rustling like a dog in the grass. As he ran a thought came into his mind.

I wish I had a dog. Running would be more fun with a dog.

The way home wound through a spinney of trees. It was autumn and the trees were like bonfires, burning arrows, and fountains of gold. But Michael ran past without even seeing them.

'I wish I had a dog,' he said aloud in time to his running.

The trees heard him and rustled to each other.

'A dog with a whisking tail,' Michael added.

The wind ran past him. Michael tried to whistle to it, but the wind is nobody's dog and goes only where it wants to. It threw a handful of bright and stolen leaves all over Michael and went off leaping among the trees. Michael thought for a moment that he could see its tail whisking in the grass. He brushed the leaves off his shoulders.

'An orange dog with a whisking tail,' Michael went on, making up a dog out of autumn and out of the wind.

The trees rustled again as he left them behind and came on to the road. Patter, patter, patter. Something was following him.

'It's my dog,' Michael said, but he did not turn round, in case it wasn't.

Patter, patter, patter . . . At last Michael just *had* to look over his shoulder. A big, orange leaf was following him – too big to come from any tree that Michael knew. When he stopped the leaf stopped too. He went on again. Patter, patter, patter went the leaf, following him.

Some men working on the roadside laughed to see a leaf following a boy. Michael grew angry with the leaf and ran faster to get away from it. The faster he ran, the faster the leaf followed him, tumbling like an

66

autumn-tinted clown, head over heels in the stones along the roadside. No matter how he tacked and dodged on the way home, he could not lose the leaf. He crawled through a hedge – but the leaf flew over it, light and rustling. He jumped over a creek and the leaf jumped after him. What was worse, it jumped better than he did. He was glad to get home and shut the door behind him. The leaf could not get in.

Later that evening his mother went to draw the curtains. She laughed and said, 'There's such a big autumn leaf out here on the windowsill, and it's fluttering up and down like a moth trying to get at the light. It looks as if it's alive.'

'Don't let it in,' said Michael quickly. 'I think it's something horrible pretending to look like a leaf . . .'

He was glad when his mother pulled the curtains, but that night, when he lay in bed, something rustled and sighed on his own windowsill, and he knew it was the leaf.

Next day it followed him to school. As he sat at his lessons he saw it dancing like a flame out in the playground, waiting for him. When he went out to play it bounced at his heels. Michael made up his mind to trap the leaf. He chased after it, but it wouldn't let itself be caught. It crouched and then flitted away. It teased him and tricked him. Michael felt that the leaf was enjoying itself thoroughly. Everybody laughed but Michael.

At last he decided he must be under some witch's spell. I'll have to go and ask Fish-and-Chips about it, he thought. He'll know what to do.

Fish-and-Chips was an old, whiskery man who lived in a cottage by the sea. He had built it himself. The walls were made of driftwood and fishbones and it was thatched with seaweed. Fish-and-Chips was not only whiskery but wise as well. He was almost a wizard, really.

After school, instead of going home by the trees, Michael ran down on to the beach. He left a trail of foot-marks behind him in the soft sand and the leaf skipped happily in and out of them. Once it rushed down to the sea to taste the salt water. Once it sailed up to where the sand ended and the grass began, but all the time it was really following Michael closely.

Fish-and-Chips was sitting at the door of his house. Michael went right up to him, but the leaf stayed a short distance away, playing by itself and watching them.

'Ah,' said Fish-and-Chips, 'I see you are being haunted. Do you want me to help you?'

'Yes please,' said Michael. 'That leaf has been following me since yesterday.'

'It must like you,' Fish-and-Chips remarked.

'But I don't want it,' Michael said. 'Can you catch it?'

'Oh yes, I think so,' Fish-and-Chips replied. 'It seems friendly and full of curiosity. Let us hide behind the door and see if it comes after us.'

They hid behind the door with the brooms, gumboots, raincoats and milk bottles all belonging to Fish-and-Chips. Through the crack in the door Michael could see the leaf coming closer and closer. It hesitated on the threshold of the cabin and then came in.

'Now!' said Fish-and-Chips, and Michael slammed the door shut while Fish-and-Chips jumped out and caught the leaf. Michael saw it twisting for a moment in his brown hands as if he were holding a little fire. Then Fish-and-Chips opened a big box and dropped the leaf in. The lid slammed down. The big orange leaf was shut up, alone in the dark.

'It won't trouble you again,' Fish-and-Chips told him.

'Thank you very much,' Michael said politely. 'How much do I owe you?'

'Whistle a sea shanty for me,' Fish-and-Chips replied. 'Whistle it into this bottle and I'll be able to use it again some time.'

So Michael whistled 'What Shall We Do with a Drunken Sailor' into the bottle. Then Fish-and-Chips corked it up quickly before the tune had time to get out. As Michael left he was writing a label for it.

Michael slowly started off home across the beach. All the time he was listening to hear the rustling of the leaf behind him. He kept looking back over his shoulder. Halfway across the beach he stopped. The beach looked empty without the bright leaf tossing behind him. He thought of it shut in that dark box in the seaweed-and-fishbones cabin. How it would hate being boxed up. Suddenly he found he was missing the leaf. Michael took one more step and then he turned round and went back to Fish-and-Chips's cabin.

Fish-and-Chips was putting the bottle up on a high shelf.

'What, more leaves already?' he asked.

'Well, no actually,' Michael said in a small voice. 'I just decided I wanted the old one back after all.'

'Oh well,' said Fish-and-Chips. 'Often people do want them back, but they don't often get them back, not quite the same. They change, you know.'

'Change?' asked Michael.

Fish-and-Chips opened his box. Out jumped a big orange dog with a whisking tail.

'Like that,' said Fish-and-Chips.

The dog put its paws on Michael's chest and licked his face.

'My dog!' Michael cried. 'It's my dog!'

He took its paws in his hands and they danced until the fishbones rattled.

'Thank you, thank you!' Michael called to Fish-and-Chips.

'Don't thank me,' Fish-and-Chips said. 'You did it all by coming back for your leaf. That's the way with magic. But just get out of my cabin before you shake the fishbones down.'

Michael leaped out through the door and ran off along the beach. The dog came bounding after him and they set off home. As they ran under the trees, leaves fell over them like a shower of gold. The wind tried to join in the chase, but Michael and his dog were too fast for it.

Trying to pretend it did not care, the wind made itself a bright scarf out of the fallen leaves and watched Michael and his autumn dog speed up the road, burrow through the hedge, jump the creek and come home at last. Laughing to itself, the wind leaped into a shining bush and sat there rustling like a salamander in the heart of a fire.

The Farmer and the Goddess

ROSALIND KERVEN

There was a young farmer who was terribly poor and terribly lonely. Although he toiled and sweated all day and half the night, he could get scarcely any crops at all to grow on his dried-up patch of land. In fact, the task would have been impossible without his ox. This animal was strong and good-natured. It pulled the plough for him; its dung helped to fertilize the wretched earth; and it was also his only companion.

One evening, the farmer was wearily making the ox comfortable for the night before settling down himself, when he let out a long, sad sigh.

At once, a voice said, 'Whatever is the matter, old friend?'

The young man jumped and gazed around in alarm. 'Who's that?' he hissed into the shadows.

'It's me. Ox.'

'You?' cried the farmer. 'What . . .? Who . . .? Never! You can . . . *speak*?'

The ox took its own turn to sigh. 'Ah, friend, I've got troubles too. Listen to this, once I was actually the Ox Star and I lived up in Heaven! Yes, I thought that would surprise you. But to cut a long story short, I got into bad trouble with the other deities because I was always acting slow and stupid, and I kept making really dreadful mistakes. So in the end they banished me, sent me down to live here on Earth, and made me work for a living. What a let down!'

The farmer was astonished and upset to hear his faithful companion's story. He patted him gently, while the ox went on.

'But I must say, you have always been very kind to me. Although you expect me to do all the heaviest work, you're always by my side and do more than your fair share. And you feed me well and always give me nice clean straw to sleep on. As punishments go, mine has been pretty easy going, thanks to you. So look, friend, why don't you tell me what's upsetting you? I'd like to help you in return, if I possibly can.'

The young man was lost for words for a few moments. Then he said, 'Ox, I can cope with most of my misfortunes. The thing that really gets me down is the utter loneliness of my life. What I want more than anything is to get married. But there's no chance of any decent woman taking a fancy to a fellow as poor and ragged as me.'

The ox gave a warm rumble of laughter. 'Oh, the solution to that couldn't be easier! Have you heard of the Heavenly Maidens? No? Well, listen carefully. You know that on the edge of the forest there's that big, beautiful lake? Well, almost every night it's visited by these wonderful young ladies – real goddesses, straight from Heaven. They come down for a swim, you see, to get away for a while from all the petty rules and restrictions up there. Now then, if you go spy on them, and hide the clothes of the one you like best while she's splashing about, I can guarantee she'll fall madly in love with you. How about that, eh?'

The young farmer had never been so excited. The next evening he finished work early for the first time in ages. He had a good wash and brush up. Then he set off for the lake and hid in the bushes.

Very soon, he saw a dazzling shower of starlight. A crowd of young women came tumbling out of it, all laughing and chattering. They threw off their clothes and, in great merriment, plunged into the water. The farmer watched, goggle-eyed.

They all looked so lovely! – much too good for him. But soon he found his eyes and his heart drawn to one who seemed quieter and gentler than the others.

His heart pounding, silently, slowly, he crept round the shore, found her clothes and snatched them away.

After some time, the Heavenly Maidens all climbed out of the water, got dressed and, one by one, rose back into the sky.

But the lady whose clothes he had stolen was left behind, alone. She wrapped her long black hair around herself, sank to the ground, and burst into tears.

At that point, the farmer plucked up courage to come out of hiding and speak to her. They talked all through the long night. She told him she was the Goddess of Weaving, but she hated living in Heaven because of her grandfather, who was unbearably strict. He told her she was the nicest person he had ever met. By the time morning broke, they had indeed fallen madly in love with each other. She was very keen to stay on Earth with him, and to get married.

So they did, and very happy they were too. The goddess carried on with her weaving work, which she was very proud of. People were queuing up to buy her beautiful cloth, so she earned plenty of money for the two of them. They used this to buy some better farm land (not forgetting a smart new shed for the good old ox to sleep in). Now they weren't poor any more. Soon they had two lovely children, a son and a daughter, and their happiness knew no bounds.

But – oh misery! – up in Heaven, the Weaving Goddess's severe old grandfather was stirring up trouble. He stomped around, shouting that a girl had no right to choose a husband for herself. He raged on and on about the disgrace she had brought upon her family by marrying a mere mortal, especially one who was so poor. And how dare she misuse her divine weaving skills to earn *money* – like a mortal peasant woman!

He went on and on about it, until his complaints reached the Jade Emperor himself. At this point, matters were taken out of his hands.

A detachment of Heavenly Guards was rushed down to Earth. Without delay, they seized the goddess out of her own home, took her prisoner, and flew her straight up to Heaven!

The farmer and their two children were there and saw everything. But no ordinary mortal can possibly stop the soldiers of the gods. The family were distraught with grief.

As they tried to comfort each other, the old ox began bellowing urgently from his stall. The farmer ran to him.

'Look,' said the ox, 'whatever you do, don't despair. Instead, go and fetch the two largest baskets you can find, quick as you can. Pop your children into them, tie them on to the ends of a pole, and hitch the lot up on to your shoulders. Then grab hold of my tail, all shut your eyes – and I'll do the rest.'

The farmer rushed off to do as the ox said. No sooner were they all ready with their eyes shut than – wooosh! – they found the ox whisking them up through the sky and heading for Heaven.

Faster and higher they rose. Soon they could see the heavy gates of Heaven looming just ahead. On the other side, the gentle goddess was probably struggling with the guards. Any minute now, they would be able to see her . . .

But they had been spotted! Every soldier in Heaven was already on emergency alert to keep them out; and at that very moment, the Jade Emperor was rising from his throne.

The Jade Emperor stretched out his hand. In a flash, he had created a broad river of stars right across the sky. It was the Milky Way.

The Weaving Goddess was stranded on one side;

the farmer and their children on the other. It was as wide as eternity; and there was no way across.

The farmer buried his head in his hands and wept. But his little daughter said, 'Father, I have found a ladle in my basket. Why don't we use it to scoop all the water out of this river?'

Although the idea was quite hopeless, the unhappy farmer seized upon it at once. The children jumped down from their baskets to help, scooping out more water with their bare hands.

But the Milky Way went on flowing, fast and deep, fast and deep.

However, when the Jade Emperor saw what they were trying to do in their desperation, even his cold heart melted a little.

He turned the farmer and the goddess each into an especially bright star, one on either side of the Milky Way. The children became two smaller stars next to their father. You can still see them all up there if you look.

Then he issued a special decree, allowing them to visit each other once a year, on the seventh day of the seventh month. That's when all the magpies on Earth fly up into the sky. They make a bridge across the Milky Way, and the little family run across it into each other's arms. Then, for a short time, they remember how happy they used to be, and the gentle goddess makes rain fall on the Earth she loves, as she weeps many tears of joy.

Send Three and Fourpence, We Are Going to a Dance

JAN MARK

Mike and Ruth Dixon got on well enough, but not so well that they wanted to walk home from school together. Ruth would not have minded, but Mike, who was two classes up, preferred to amble along with his friends so that he usually arrived a long while after Ruth did.

Ruth was leaning out of the kitchen window when he came in through the side gate, kicking a brick.

'I've got a message for you,' said Mike. 'From school. Miss Middleton wants you to go and see her tomorrow before assembly, and take a dead frog.'

'What's she want *me* to take a dead frog for?' said Ruth. 'She's not my teacher. I haven't got a dead frog.'

'How should I know?' Mike let himself in. 'Where's Mum?'

'Round Mrs Todd's. Did she really say a dead frog? I mean, really say it?'

'Derek told me to tell you. It's nothing to do with me.'

Ruth cried easily. She cried now. 'I bet she never. You're pulling my leg.'

'I'm not, and you'd better do it. She said it was important – Derek said – and you know what a rotten old temper she's got,' said Mike feelingly.

'But why me? It's not fair.' Ruth leaned her head on the windowsill and wept in earnest. 'Where'm I going to find a dead frog?'

'Well, you can peel them off the road sometimes, when they've been run over. They go all dry and flat, like pressed flowers,' said Mike. He did think it a trifle unreasonable to demand dead frogs from little girls, but Miss Middleton *was* unreasonable. Everyone knew that. 'You could start a pressed frog collection,' he said.

Ruth sniffed fruitily. 'What do you think Miss'll do if I don't get one?'

'She'll go barmy, that's what,' said Mike. 'She's

barmy anyway,' he said. 'Nah, don't start howling again. Look, I'll go down the ponds after tea. I know there's frogs there because I saw the spawn, back at Easter.'

'But those frogs are alive. She wants a dead one.'

'I dunno. Perhaps we could get it put to sleep or something, like Mrs Todd's Tibby was. And don't tell Mum. She doesn't like me down the ponds and she won't let us have frogs indoors. Get an old box with a lid and leave it on the rockery, and I'll put old Froggo in it when I come home. *And stop crying!*'

After Mike had gone out, Ruth found the box that her summer sandals had come in. She poked air holes in the top and furnished it with damp grass and a tin lid full of water. Then she left it on the rockery with a length of darning wool so that Froggo could be fastened down safely until morning. It was only possible to imagine Froggo alive; all tender and green and saying croak-croak. She could not think of him dead and flat and handed over to Miss Middleton, who definitely must have gone barmy. Perhaps Mike or Derek had been wrong about the dead part. She hoped they had.

She was in the bathroom, getting ready for bed, when Mike came home. He looked round the door and stuck up his thumbs.

'Operation Frog successful. Over and out.'

'Wait. Is he . . . alive?'

'Shhh. Mum's in the hall. Yes.'

'What's he like?'

'Sort of frog-shaped. Look, I've got him OK? I'm going down now.'

'Is he green?'

'No. More like that pork pie that went mouldy on top. Goodnight!'

Mike had hidden Froggo's dungeon under the front hedge, so all Ruth had to do next morning was scoop it up as she went out of the gate. Mike had left earlier with his friends, so she paused for a moment to introduce herself. She tapped quietly on the lid. 'Hello?'

There was no answering cry of croak-croak. Perhaps he *was* dead. Ruth felt a tear coming and raised the lid a fraction at one end. There was a scrabbling noise and at the other end of the box she saw something small and alive, crouching in the grass.

'Poor Froggo,' she whispered through the air holes. 'I won't let her kill you, I promise,' and she continued on her way to school feeling brave and desperate, and ready to protect Froggo's life at the cost of her own.

The school hall was in the middle of the building and classrooms opened off it. Miss Middleton had

Class 3 this year, next to the cloakroom. Ruth hung up her blazer, untied the wool from Froggo's box, and went to meet her doom. Miss Middleton was arranging little stones in an aquarium on top of the bookcase, and jerked her head when Ruth knocked, to show that she should come in.

'I got him, Miss,' said Ruth, holding out the shoe box in trembling hands.

'What, dear?' said Miss Middleton, up to her wrists in water-weed.

'Only he's not dead and I won't let you kill him!' Ruth cried, and swept off the lid with a dramatic flourish. Froggo, who must have been waiting for this, sprung out towards Miss Middleton, landed with a clammy sound on that vulnerable place between the collar bones, and slithered down inside Miss Middleton's blouse.

Miss Middleton taught Nature Study. She was not afraid of little damp creatures, but she was not expecting Froggo. She gave a squawk of alarm and jumped backwards. The aquarium skidded in the opposite direction, took off, shattered against a desk. The contents broke over Ruth's new sandals in a tidal wave, and Lily the goldfish thrashed about in a shallow puddle on the floor. People came running with mops and dustpans. Lily Fish was taken out by the tail to recover in the cloakroom sink. Froggo was arrested while trying to leave Miss Middleton's blouse through the gap between two buttons, and put back in his box with a weight on top in case he made another dash for freedom.

Ruth, crying harder than she had ever done in her life, was sent to stand outside the headmaster's room, accused of playing stupid practical jokes and cruelty to frogs.

Sir looked rather as if he had been laughing, but it seemed unlikely under the circumstances, and Ruth's eyes were so swollen and tear-filled that she couldn't see clearly. He gave her a few minutes to dry out and then said, 'This isn't like you, Ruth. Whatever possessed you to go throwing frogs at poor Miss Middleton? And poor frog, come to that.'

'She told me to bring her a frog,' said Ruth, staunching another tear at the injustice of it all. 'Only she wanted a dead one, and I couldn't find a dead one, and I couldn't kill Froggo. I won't kill him,' she said, remembering her view on the way to school.

'Miss Middleton says she did not ask you to bring her a frog, or kill her a frog. She thinks you've been very foolish and unkind,' said Sir, 'and I think you are not telling the truth. Now . . .'

'Mike told me to,' said Ruth.

'Your brother? Oh, come now.'

'He did. He said Miss Middleton wanted me to go to her before assembly with a dead frog and I did, only it wasn't dead and I won't!'

'Ruth! Don't grizzle. No one is going to murder your frog, but we must get this nonsense sorted out.' Sir opened his door and called to a passer-by, 'Tell Michael Dixon that I want to see him at once, in my office.'

Mike arrived, looking wary. He had heard the crash and kept out of the way, but a summons from Sir was not to be ignored.

'Come in, Michael,' said Sir. 'Now, why did you tell your sister that Miss Middleton wanted her to bring a dead frog to school?'

'It wasn't me,' said Mike. 'It was a message from Miss Middleton.'

'Miss Middleton told you?'

'No, Derek Bingham told me. She told him to tell me – I suppose,' said Mike sulkily. He scowled at Ruth. All her fault.

'Then you'd better fetch Derek Bingham here right away. We're going to get to the bottom of this.'

Derek arrived. He too had heard the crash.

'Come in, Derek,' said Sir. 'I understand that you

told Michael here some tarradiddle about his sister. You let him think it was a message from Miss Middleton, didn't you?'

'Yes, well . . .' Derek shuffled. 'Miss Middleton didn't tell *me*. She told, er, someone, and they told me.'

'Who was this someone?'

Derek turned all noble and stood up straight and pale. 'I can't remember, Sir.'

'Don't let's have any heroics about sneaking, Derek, or I shall get very *cross*.'

Derek's nobility ebbed rapidly. 'It was Tim Hancock, Sir. He said Miss Middleton wanted Ruth Dixon to bring her a dead dog before assembly.'

'A dead *dog*?'

'Yes, Sir.'

'Didn't you think it a bit strange that Miss Middleton should ask Ruth for a dead dog, Derek?'

'I thought she must have one, Sir.'

'But why should Miss Middleton want it?'

'Well, she does do Nature Study,' said Derek.

'Go and fetch Tim,' said Sir.

Tim had been playing football on the field when the aquarium went down. He came in with an innocent smile which wilted when he saw what was waiting for him.

'Sir?'

'Would you mind repeating the message that you gave Derek yesterday afternoon?'

'I told him Miss Middleton wanted Sue Nixon to bring her a red sock before assembly,' said Tim. 'It was important.'

'Red sock? Sue Nixon?' said Sir. He was beginning to look slightly wild-eyed. 'Who's Sue Nixon? There's no one in this school called Sue Nixon.'

'I don't know any of the girls, Sir,' said Tim.

'Didn't you think a red sock was an odd thing to ask for?'

'I thought she was bats, Sir.'

'Sue Nixon?'

'No, Sir. Miss Middleton, Sir,' said truthful Tim.

Sir raised his eyebrows. 'But why did you tell Derek?'

'I couldn't find anyone else, Sir. It was late.'

'But why Derek?'

'I had to tell someone or I'd have got into trouble,' said Tim virtuously.

'You are in trouble,' said Sir. 'Michael, ask Miss Middleton to step in here for a moment, please.'

Miss Middleton, frog-ridden, looked round the door.

'I'm sorry to bother you again,' said Sir, 'but it seems that Tim thinks you told him that one Sue Nixon was to bring you a red sock before assembly.'

'Tim!' said Miss Middleton, very shocked. 'That's a naughty fib. I never told you any such thing.'

'Oh Sir,' said Tim. 'Miss didn't tell me. It was Pauline Bates done that.'

'*Did* that. I think I see Pauline out in the hall,' said Sir. 'In the PT class. Yes? Let's have her in.'

Pauline was very small and very frightened. Sir sat her on his knee and told her not to worry. 'All we want to know,' he said, 'is what you said to Tim yesterday. About Sue Nixon and the dead dog.'

'Red sock, Sir,' said Tim.

'Sorry. Red sock. Well, Pauline?'

Pauline looked as if she might join Ruth in tears. Ruth had just realized that she was no longer involved, and was crying with relief.

'You said Miss Middleton gave you a message for Sue Nixon. What was it?'

'It wasn't Sue Nixon,' said Pauline, damply. 'It was June Nichols. It wasn't Miss Middleton, it was Miss Wimbledon.'

'There *is* no Miss Wimbledon,' said Sir. 'June Nichols, yes. I know June, but Miss Wimbledon . . .?'

'She means Miss Wimpole, Sir,' said Tim. 'The

89

big girls call her Wimbledon 'cause she plays tennis, Sir, in a little skirt.'

'I thought you didn't know any girls,' said Sir. 'What did Miss Wimpole say to you, Pauline?'

'She didn't,' said Pauline. 'It was Moira Thatcher. She said to tell June Nichols to come and see Miss Whatsit before assembly and bring her bed socks.'

'Then why tell Tim?'

'I couldn't find June. June's in his class.'

'I begin to see daylight,' said Sir. 'Not much, but it's there. All right, Pauline. Go and get Moira, please.'

Moira had recently had a new brace fitted across her front teeth. It caught the light when she opened her mouth.

'Yeth, Their?'

'Moira, take it slowly, and tell us what the message was about June Nichols.'

Moira took a deep breath and polished the brace with her tongue.

'Well, Their, Mith Wimpole thaid to tell June to thee her before athembly with her wed fw – thw – thth –'

'Frock?' said Sir. Moira nodded gratefully. 'So why tell Pauline?'

'Pauline liveth up her thtweet, Their.'

'No I don't,' said Pauline. 'They moved. They got a council house, up the Ridgeway.'

'All right, Moira,' said Sir. 'Just ask Miss Wimpole if she could thp – spare me a minute of her time, please?'

If Miss Wimpole was surprised to find eight people in Sir's office, she didn't show it. As there was no longer room to get inside, she stood at the doorway and waved. Sir waved back. Mike instantly decided that Sir fancied Miss Wimpole.

'Miss Wimpole, I believe you must be the last link in the chain. Am I right in thinking that you wanted June Nichols to see you before assembly, with her red frock?'

'Why, yes,' said Miss Wimpole. 'She's dancing a solo at the end–of–term concert. I wanted her to practise, but she didn't turn up.'

'Thank you,' said Sir. 'One day, when we both have a spare hour or two, I'll tell you why she didn't turn up. As for you lot,' he said, turning to the mob round his desk, 'you seem to have been playing Chinese Whispers without knowing it. You also seem to think that the entire staff is off its head. You may be right. I don't know. Red socks, dead dogs, live frogs – we'll put your friend in the school pond, Ruth. Fetch him at break. And now, someone had better find

June Nichols and deliver Miss Wimpole's message.'

'Oh, there's no point, Sir. She couldn't have come anyway,' said Ruth. 'She's got chicken-pox. She hasn't been at school for ages.'

Kylie and the
Can-Can Beans

CAROLINE PITCHER

Kylie could hear strange music floating across the supermarket. She began to dance. Her mother called, 'If someone's already taken an orange to school, you could take a fig, grow a tree from the seeds and all eat fresh figs.'

'Eugh! Dees-GUST-ing,' sang Kylie, and waltzed away past a little boy yanking the handle of the chocolate raisin dispenser. Chocolate raisins hailstoned into his hands and bounced on the supermarket floor.

'Want some?' he cried, offering her a sticky handful.

'No thanks,' said Kylie. The music led her in a dance right up to a basket labelled 'ODD FRUIT. REDUCED'. In the basket was a soggy kiwi fruit, a bruised yellow pear and something else. It looked like a prickly pink egg.

'MUM!' screamed Kylie. 'I've found it.'

The music stopped at once.

'No one else'll take an Odd Fruit to grow!' cried Kylie. 'Mine'll be special!'

After all, everyone else in Mrs Poon's class was special at something.

Dianne danced dainty as a sugar strand in her pink ballerina's dress, but when Kylie went to the dance class in her orange leotard, Dianne sniffed, 'I didn't know pumpkins could dance.'

Kylie's friend Janey swam like a dolphin. Kylie sank every few strokes, like a bathtime whale without its bung.

Penny played the 'Moonlight Sonata' on the piano in Assembly. Kylie played 'Chopsticks'. Wrong.

'This time it'll be different,' said Kylie.

When Kylie opened the Odd Fruit at home she pricked her finger.

'Perhaps it's a Sleeping Beauty Fruit,' she said. 'A prince will give me a smacking great kiss. I know it's a special fruit, Mum.'

'It's a revolting fruit,' grumbled her mum. 'I'm not surprised it's cheap.'

Inside, the fruit was all sludgy and tasted like curried wellies. In the middle were lots and lots of seeds shaped like big baked beans.

They were pink.

'If we soak some of these seeds they will germinate quickly,' said Mum. 'And we can dry the rest to make necklaces, just like you can with melon seeds.'

Kylie had never made a melon-seed necklace in her life and did not intend to start now, but she liked to keep her mother happy, so she said, 'I'll dry them in a paper bag, Mum.' She stuffed the bag in the WHERE-ELSE-CAN-I-PUT-IT drawer. This drawer was next to the boiler and it was crammed full of rubber bands, past-it pens, some smelly sheep's wool and a couple of teeth, a gang of Rice Krispie men, yellowed curtain hooks and a cola lolly Kylie had started last Christmas.

She put the six biggest beans in a yoghurt pot and covered them with water, and the next morning she carried the pot to school as carefully as if it were a casket of rubies. She couldn't wait to see what grew from them!

Mrs Poon peered at the pink beans in the pot.

'I've never heard of an Odd Fruit before,' she said.

'Well done, Kylie. Help yourself to a plant pot and some compost.'

Kylie planted her six seeds lovingly, kissing her finger and pressing the kiss on each little bean as she shoved it down into the compost.

She daydreamed that six beautiful trees grew, with flowers like honeyed trumpets and plump pink fruit. In the dream, Kylie handed out fruit to all the grateful children, who cried, 'Thank you, kind Kylie, oh thank you!'

And the Dream Fruit tasted delicious, a mingling of sweet melon, strawberry and chocolate.

In the classroom, Lucy's lychee grew a shoot, Annie's avocado grew roots and a strong red stalk. Sidney's satsuma sprouted and so did Errol's pink grapefruit.

Shoots sprang from lemons and limes, apples and pears, melons and mangos. Something grew in every pot.

Every little pot except Kylie's, so she hid it at the back.

'Perhaps the compost is too dry,' said Mrs Poon.

Kylie filled the saucer to the very brim with water.

Nothing happened.

'Perhaps the compost is too wet,' said Mrs Poon.

Kylie tipped the water away.

Nothing happened.

On Friday, Kylie carried her pot home with her hand over the top pretending she was protecting a new and delicate shoot, but as soon as she was home she hurled the whole thing into the dustbin and slammed down the lid. Then she ran inside, weeping noisily.

'I believed you were special, Odd Fruit,' she sobbed. 'And you let me down! Nothing ever goes right for me!'

She grabbed some biscuits from the tin and sat down. In the corner of the kitchen the television picture flickered. Kylie scowled at it through her tears. A skinny woman was tilling dusty grey ground. A little boy with nutmeg skin and a belly like a pudding basin trailed along behind her. A voice told viewers how a group called Watering Can was trying to help, because it was so difficult to grow things when there was hardly any rain.

'I know, mate,' said Kylie sympathetically. 'I can't grow nothing even when I have got water.'

The little boy turned and stared. His dark eyes welled with sadness. Kylie remembered the boy in the supermarket, laughing as he guzzled chocolate raisins.

'All *you've* got to eat is dust,' said Kylie.

She put her biscuits back in the tin.

On Saturday morning, Kylie got up late. Mum was washing up while jolly dance music blared out of the radio. There were trumpets and saxophones, a double bass, drums, and whisking rhythm noises, and a lot of tap-tapping.

The music stopped.

The tap-tapping didn't.

'Mum, we've got mice,' shrieked Kylie. 'They're in that drawer, the WHERE-ELSE-CAN-I-PUT-IT drawer. I can hear their little feet.'

Kylie crept up to the drawer. She hesitated and then slid the drawer open, oh so slowly. A brown paper bag was wriggling around inside.

'Eh? What's in there?' cried Kylie. 'Must be a body-popping spider!'

She snatched up the bag and shook it. Out fell six pink beans. The beans got up on long long legs and made themselves into a chorus line.

The music played and the beans began to dance.

How they danced! They high-kicked to the left, then high-kicked to the right, and then the chorus line split in the middle and formed a wheel, facing different ways, and circled round, kicking all together.

'Wow!' screamed Kylie. 'They can kick even higher than themselves!'

The beans had tufty pink hair on the top of

their heads and tiny silver high-heeled dance shoes.

'Their legs are really roots,' cried Kylie. 'They must have sprung in that drawer 'cos it's near the boiler and it's warm. They didn't need water or soil after all.'

'They're dancing the Can-Can,' whispered Mum.

'All except that one,' said Kylie.

At the end of the chorus line one very big bean sat in a heap with her roots all over the place as if she had collapsed, out of breath.

'She looks like Humpty Dumpty fallen off the wall,' giggled Kylie. 'I shall call her Betty.'

Over the weekend, Mum made a tape of dance music specially for the beans and the instant Kylie switched it on the beans burst into their dance routine.

'Now, Mum, I need your help,' announced Kylie. 'I think I've got these beans for a purpose.'

'What do you mean?' said Mum.

'I'll tell you as we go along,' said Kylie.

Kylie and her mum made a theatre from a box. There was a large stage for the seeds to dance on. Mum made blue velvet curtains tied back with silver ribbons. 'We better not dress 'em up, we might damage 'em so they'd have to retire from the stage for ever,' warned Kylie.

Kylie made happy and sad theatre masks and coloured them with her gold pen. She stuck these above the stage. She cut out tickets and sliced a slot in the top of an empty golden syrup tin to collect money. Then Kylie made a poster.

KYLIE'S AMAZING CAN-CAN BEANS
will perform
every Wednesday and Friday lunchtime.
VENUE
Mrs Poon's room
ADMISSION
Juniors twenty-five pence
Infants fifteen pence
Nursery kids five pence

''Cos they don't take up much room,' explained Kylie before the show. 'The money's not for me. I thought I couldn't grow anything. Now the beans and me are going to make money for a little boy and his mum and the people who can't grow anything to eat. The money's for wells for water to drink, and for watering their vegetables.'

The beans gave a brilliant performance. The children gasped with wonder, and Mrs Poon clapped her hands with joy, and cried, 'They're fantastic. But what's the matter with that plump one? Has it got a headache?'

'That's Betty,' explained Kylie.

After school, Kylie's mum said, 'Don't work the dance troupe too hard. They look tired. Betty's exhausted. She looks as if she's propped up on one elbow and she's getting even fatter. Put her in the airing cupboard where it's warm.'

So Kylie lay Betty on a towel on the top shelf where it was warm and dark and peaceful. The other five beans rested in a shoe box lined with pink cotton wool.

Kylie's Can-Can Beans gave performances at school, a performance at the library on Saturday morning, and a performance at the local Summer Fair. They got better and better. They put new dances into their repertoire, the tango and River Dance. People shouted BRAVO and ENCORE, especially when they danced to 'Hello Dolly' down gold cardboard steps.

Kylie counted the money like an old Scrooge. Her mum changed it for a cheque so that it wouldn't burst the envelope. Then Kylie wrote the letter to the charity:

'Dear Watering Can,

Here is fifty pounds three pence I collected from concerts that my Dancing Beans gave. I hope you'll use the money to help people grow things and show them how to get well.

Love, Kylie and her Can-Can Beans.'

She soon received a letter back from Watering Can thanking her and telling her to thank the seeds, which she did, of course. There were photos of dry dusty land, then of it being dug and irrigated, then of people planting and harvesting crops. There was one photo of a little boy grinning at a big bowl full of vegetables.

'I bet you're the same little boy off the telly,' Kylie whispered to him. 'I'm glad your tummy is full at last.'

Kylie was so happy. She felt full of power.

'Much better than playing a stupid violin or winning sistificates,' cried Kylie. 'I think I'll be a fundraiser when I grow up.'

'Let the beans rest until Christmas now,' said Mum after the seeds had danced at their holiday camp. 'They look tired.'

'Yes, I'll put them away in their drawer,' said Kylie. 'They can give more shows at Christmas. I'll make a tinful of money then, people feel kind.'

But those seeds never did dance at Christmas.

Winter came early, in November. It snowed as thick and white as icing on a Christmas cake.

'Ooooh! I'd better show the beans,' said Kylie. 'They've never seen snow before.'

And she opened the drawer, took out the shoe box and gasped.

There lay her dance troupe, dried up, shrivelled, withered. Dead.

'They'll never dance again,' cried Kylie. 'Look at their little rooty legs stuck up in the air, like dead budgies' legs at the bottom of a cage.'

'Don't cry, Kylie,' sobbed her mum. 'It's the end of their life cycle. It's only natural. You know, "to everything there is a season . . . a time to love . . . a time to dance . . ."'

'Don't be so soppy, Mum,' snapped Kylie. She scooped the seeds back into the bag and dropped the whole lot in the bin.

Then she pounded upstairs, flung open the door of the airing cupboard, stretched up and groped around on the top shelf.

It was just as she'd thought.

Betty wasn't just a fat pink bean any more. She had grown into a big pink fruit with soft new prickles.

'You're not a Has-Bean, Betty. You're the Queen Bean,' cried Kylie.

She put Betty to her ear and shook her, oh so gently. She could hear lots of little beans jigging around inside.

'Well hello, Daughters of Betty,' cried Kylie. 'I look forward to your first show in the spring. We're still in business, Can-Can Beans!'

How the Badger Got Its Stripes

TERRY JONES

In the great long-ago, the badger was pure white all over.

'How sorry I feel for the bear with his dull brown coat,' the badger would say. 'And who would want to be like Leopard – all covered in spots? Or – worse still – like Tiger, with his vulgar striped coat! I am glad that the Maker of All Things gave me this pure white coat without a blemish on it!'

This is how the badger would boast as he paraded through the forest, until all the other creatures were thoroughly sick and tired of him.

'He always looks down his nose at me,' said the rabbit, 'because only my tail is white.'

'And he sneers at me,' said the field mouse, 'because I'm such a mousy colour.'

'And he calls me an eye-sore!' exclaimed the zebra.

'It's time we put a stop to it,' they said.

'Then may I make a suggestion?' asked the fox, and he outlined a plan to which all the other animals agreed.

Some time later, the fox went to the badger and said, 'O, Badger, please help us! You are, without doubt, the best-looking creature in the Wild Wood. It's not just your coat (which is exceedingly beautiful and without a blemish) but it is also . . . oh . . . the way you walk on your hind legs . . . the way you hold your head up . . . your superb manners and graceful ways . . . Won't you help us humbler animals by giving us lessons in how to improve our looks and how to carry ourselves?'

Well, the badger was thrilled to hear all these compliments and he replied very graciously, 'Of course, my dear Fox. I'll see what I can do.'

So the fox called all the animals to meet in the Great Glade, and said to them, 'Badger, here, has kindly agreed to give us lessons in how to look as handsome as he does. He will also instruct us in etiquette, deportment and fashion.'

There were one or two sniggers amongst the smaller animals at this point, but the badger didn't notice. He stood up on his hind legs, puffed himself up with pride, and said, 'I am very happy to be in a position to help you less fortunate animals, and I must say I can see much room for improvement. You, Wolf, for example, have such a shabby coat . . .'

'But it's the only one I've got!' said the wolf.

'And I pity you, Beaver,' went on the badger, 'such an ordinary pelt you have . . . and as for that ridiculous tail . . .'

'Er, Badger,' interrupted the fox, 'rather than going through all our short-comings (interesting and instructive though that certainly may be), why don't you teach us how to walk with our noses in the air – the way that makes you look so distinguished and sets off your beautiful unblemished white coat so well?'

'By all means,' said the badger.

'Why not walk to the other end of the Glade, so we can see?' said the fox.

'Certainly,' said the badger. And so, without suspecting a thing, he started to walk to the other end of the Glade.

Now, if the badger had not been so blinded by his

own self-satisfaction, he might have noticed the rat and the stoat and the weasel smirking behind their paws. And if he had looked a little closer, he might have noticed a twinkle in many an animal's eye. But he didn't. He just swaggered along on his hind legs with his nose right up in the air, saying, 'This is the way to walk . . . notice how gracefully I raise my back legs . . . and see how I am always careful to keep my brush well ooooooooaaaarrrggggghhhup!'

This is the moment that the badger discovered the fox's plan. The fox had got all the other animals to dig a deep pit at one end of the Great Glade. This they had filled with muddy water and madder-root, and then covered it over with branches and fern.

The badger, with his nose in the air, had of course walked straight into it – feet first. And he sank in – right up to his neck.

'Help!' he cried. 'Help! My beautiful white coat! Please pull me out, someone! Help!'

Well, of course, all the animals in the Glade laughed and pointed at the poor badger as he struggled to keep his head out of the muck. Eventually he had to pull himself out by his own efforts.

When the badger looked down at his beautiful white coat, stained with mud and madder-root, he was so mortified that he ran off out of the forest with a pitiful howl. And he ran and he ran until he came to a lake of crystal water.

There he tried to clean the stuff off his coat, but madder-root is a powerful dye, and no matter what he did, he could not get it off.

'What shall I do?' he moaned to himself. 'My beautiful white coat . . . my pride and joy . . . ruined for ever! How can I hold my head up in the forest again?'

To make matters worse, at that moment, a creature whom the badger had never seen before swam up to him and said: 'What are you doing – washing your filthy old coat in our crystal-clear lake? Push off!'

The badger was speechless – not only because he wasn't used to being spoken to like this, but also because the creature had such a beautiful coat. It was as white and unblemished as the badger's own coat used to be.

'Who are you?' asked the badger.

'I'm Swan, of course,' replied the swan. 'Now shove off! We don't want dirty creatures like you around here!' And the swan rose up on its legs and beat its powerful wings, and the badger slunk away on all fours, with his tail between his legs.

For the rest of the day, the badger hid himself away in a grove overlooking the crystal lake. From there, he gazed down at the white swan, gliding proudly about the lake, and the badger was so filled with bitterness and envy that he thought he would burst.

That very night, however, he stole down to the swan's nest when the swan was fast asleep and very, very gently he pulled out one of the swan's feathers and then scuttled back to his hiding-place.

He did the same thing the next night, and the next and the next, and each night he returned to the grove, where he was busy making himself a new coat of white feathers, to cover up his stained fur.

And, because the badger did all this so slowly and slyly, the swan never noticed, until all but one of his feathers had disappeared.

That night the swan couldn't sleep, because of the draught from where his feathers were missing, and so it was that he saw the badger creeping up to steal the last one. As he did so the swan rose up with a terrible cry. He pecked off the badger's tail and beat him with his wings and chased him off.

Then the swan returned to the crystal lake, and sat there lamenting over his lost feathers.

When the Maker of All Things found the swan – that he had made so beautiful – sitting there bald and featherless, he was extremely surprised.

But he was even more surprised when he went to the Wild Wood and found the badger parading about, looking quite ridiculous in his stolen feather coat!

'Badger!' exclaimed the Maker of All Things. 'I knew you were vain, but I didn't know you were a thief as well!'

And there and then he took the feathers and gave them back to the swan.

'From this day on,' he said to the badger, 'you will wear only your coat stained with madder-root. And, if you're going to steal, I'd better give you a thief's mask as well!'

And the Maker of All Things drew his fingers across the Badger's eyes, and left him with two black stripes – like a mask – from ears to snout.

The badger was so ashamed that he ran off and hid, and to this very day all badgers avoid company. They live in solitude, stealing a little bit here and there, wherever they can. And each and every badger still wears a mask of stripes across its eyes.

The Bag of Winds

RETOLD BY POMME CLAYTON

When the world was first made, there was no wind. No wind at all. The wind did not blow over land or sea. There was no wind to rustle the leaves or whip up the waves. There was no wind to blow away rain clouds or cool down a hot day. There was not even a ripple on the surface of the water. The sea was as still as glass. And in those days, if you wanted to travel by boat, you had to row, and it was back-breaking work.

Now, there was one sea captain who was fed up with rowing everywhere. He had heard that somewhere there was a cave and in that cave lived the winds. And these winds were so strong they could make a ship move! The captain thought that if he could find the cave and set the winds free, then he would put an end to rowing – for good.

So the captain set off over a lonely cliff top, to ask the fishwife if she knew anything about the winds. The fishwife sold fish in the streets, but her real trade was in tongue wagging. She knew all the gossip and tales of the town, and many charms and spells besides. If the fishwife didn't know about the winds, then nobody would. The captain knocked on her cottage door, and a wrinkled old woman, stinking of fish, appeared.

'Come inside, Captain,' she croaked. 'What can I do for you?'

'I want to find the winds,' said the captain, 'and set them free. Do you know where they are?'

'That's what you want, is it?' muttered the fishwife. 'Well, it's a dangerous task. The winds live far up north, in the Country of the Winds. It will be a long journey, and you will need a good ship – fitted with sails.'

'Whatever it takes,' cried the captain, 'I'm going there!'

'But that's only the beginning, bold Captain,' said

the fishwife, sucking her teeth. 'The winds are wild and you will have to tame them.'

And the fishwife reached into her apron pocket and pulled out a little wooden pipe.

'Play this pipe and the winds will grow calm. Tie them up in a strong bag and nail the bag to the mast of your ship. Then let the gentle west wind out of the bag and the wind will fill your sails and waft you home. But whatever you do, don't let any other winds out of the bag until you are safely in harbour.'

The fishwife gave the captain the little pipe. 'And good luck to you,' she said, shaking her head.

The captain walked into town, with the pipe in his pocket, and hired twenty strapping, sturdy men to be his crew. He offered each man a bag of gold at the end of the voyage, but he did not tell them where they were going. He fitted a ship with a strong mast and twenty pairs of oars. He had three large sails stitched from canvas, and he made a bag from the toughest ox-hide. He bought kegs of beer and a ton of ship's biscuits to keep the crew going. Then he turned his ship towards the north.

The crew pulled at the oars night and day. And they slowly made their way across the smooth, still water. At first it was hot, and the crew sweated and panted with the effort of rowing. But the further north they rowed, the cooler it became. They rowed north and it grew bitterly, bitterly cold. They rowed north and there were icebergs floating in the sea and sheer cliffs of snow towering above them. They rowed so far north that the sea froze and they could row no more.

The ship ran aground beside a cave made of ice. From the cave came a wild roaring and moaning sound, so terrible that even the strapping, sturdy crew shuddered. They had reached the Country of the Winds.

The captain put the ox-hide bag under his arm and tapped his pocket to make sure the pipe was still there. Then, leaving the crew to guard the boat, he climbed into the cave.

Suddenly, he was hit by something, something he could not see. It was so strong it nearly knocked him over and so angry it nearly ripped the coat from his back. It was the winds! The captain turned up his collar and peered about the cave. He could just make out the faint outlines of eight creatures, ghostly white with great wings.

They were the eight winds. And they were flying round and round the cave sucking in air and blowing it out. Some of the winds were old with trailing beards, some were young and forceful, others were bold and blasting, one was gentle and balmy. The winds swirled and swooped around each other, blowing hot and cold, wailing and whistling.

The captain pulled the wooden pipe from his pocket, put it to his lips and began to play. The pipe had a sweet clear tone and the sound soared around the cave. The winds stopped howling and listened. The pipe soothed them and, one by one, they floated softly to the ground and lay at the captain's feet. Quickly the captain opened the neck of the bag and swept all eight winds inside. Then he tied up the bag with a stout knot, carried it back to the ship and nailed it to the mast.

'Men,' he warned, 'you touch this bag on pain of death!'

The captain ordered his crew to hoist the sails. The crew had never seen sails before, and they heaved and pulled the stiff canvas up the mast in silence. Then the captain opened the bag, just a tiny bit, and caught the gentle west wind in his fist. He closed the bag swiftly and let the wind loose. The sweet west wind blew softly. The sails filled with air, and the ship began to move across the water by the sheer power of the wind. The crew were amazed! The huge sails billowed and the ship speed over the sea. All the crew had to do was steer. So they took it in turns to guide the helm, while the rest of the crew sat back and enjoyed the ride. They sang sea-shanties, told stories and dozed, and the west wind blew them safely home.

But the youngest member of the crew, the cabin boy, could not take his eyes off the strange bag nailed to the mast. There was something inside it, alive and kicking and struggling to get out. The cabin boy longed to know what it was. He looked about the deck, the crew were all busy or asleep, and he thought to himself, No one will notice if I take a peep.

So he crept up to the mast, untied the knot, opened the neck of the bag and looked inside. Suddenly, there was a great rush and something white like a ghost burst out of the bag. The cabin boy was terrified and he quickly tied up the knot. But it was too late, for he had let out the terrible south-west wind. Instantly the south-west wind filled his cheeks with air and began to blow with all his might. He roared and bellowed and blew up a gale. He whipped up huge waves and water washed over the side of the boat. The south-west wind blew so hard that the ship was lifted right up into the air. A whirlwind spun the ship round and round, then a great gust of wind dashed the ship down on to a rock. The ship smashed into a thousand pieces. The crew and the captain and the cabin boy were all swept into the cold water and drowned.

As the boat broke apart, the bag split open and out flew the other winds. Now the eight winds were free and that night, there was the first storm at sea. It was ugly weather and many boats were wrecked. The eight winds blew their way across the whole world. And they are still blowing to this very day. For no one can get the winds back into the bag.

Ever since then, a ship's crew have been called sailors – after the sails they use to trap the wind. All sailors wear sou'westers, oil-skin hats and coats, to protect them from the terrible south-west wind. And sometimes, when the sea is calm and there is no wind, sailors whistle for the wind. But they must be careful and whistle sweetly – for they never know which wind is going to come. And they might get more than they bargained for.

Spider George

ALEX SHEARER

Spider George had a bad dream, and so he woke and shouted for his mother.

'Mum, Mum!' he yelled. 'Help, come quick!'

'What is it, dear?' she said. 'Whatever is the matter?'

'Help,' said George. 'I'm frightened! There's a person in the room!'

'Oh, George,' his mother said. 'Not that again. Don't be so silly!'

'No, there is,' said George. 'There really is!'

His mother looked around the room but could not see anyone.

'Look under the chair!' George said.

She did, but could see nothing.

'It was just a dream, George, that was all.'

'It wasn't,' said George. 'I saw them! It was a nasty person. One of the horrible ones. You know – with two legs!'

'Oh, George,' his mother said. 'You're imagining it.'

'I'm not,' George said. 'It was coming to get me! Can I come and sleep in your web?'

'Well, try to get back to sleep in your own room first, George. You know when you sleep in our web that you only keep your father awake, snoring and kicking him in the back. Here, I'll tuck you in.'

So George's mother tucked him back into his web, which wasn't easy, as he had eight legs. And as soon as she got five or six of them tucked in, two or three of them would drop out. But she managed it in the end, and she put on his night-light, and at last he got back to sleep.

At breakfast next morning, George's mum said to his father, 'We're going to have to do something about George. He's frightened of people. In fact, he's got quite a phobia about them.'

'Oh, I wouldn't worry too much,' George's father said. 'He'll grow out of it. When I was his age, I used to be quite frightened of people myself. But they don't bother me now. I still don't like the really big nasty ones, but the little ones are perfectly harmless, and can even be quite useful. They're good at putting the rubbish out, and things like that.'

But no sooner had he finished speaking than there was a terrible cry, and a second later, George ran in, in a terrible state of agitation.

'Help, help,' he yelled. 'I went to use the loo, but there's a person under the toilet seat!'

'Oh, George,' his mum said. 'You're imagining it.'

'I'm not,' said George. 'There's a person in the toilet bowl. Maybe even two of them. With big teeth. Waiting to bite me on the bottom.'

'Come along, George,' his mother said. 'I'll go with you.'

And she went with him and showed him that there were no people there at all.

George played happily by himself for the rest of the morning. His mother took him to the park in the afternoon, where he practised his silk spinning among the trees. After that, he played hide and seek and musical webs with his friends, then they went home for tea.

George's mother was in the kitchen taking a packet of frozen flies out of the freezer, when she heard another scream, this time from the bathroom.

She ran there at once.

'What is it, George?' she said. 'Whatever is the matter?'

'Look,' George said. 'Look, look! There's a person in the bath! They must have come up the plughole.'

'Honestly, George, there's no one there.'

'There is!' George cried. 'They've gone now, but there *was* someone. They've gone back down the plughole, that's all. They're waiting to get me at bath time. They live down the plughole and they wait until a poor spider comes by, then they pop up and grab you. And they hit you with a newspaper. Or they pull all your legs off, just for fun.'

'Stuff and nonsense,' his mother said. 'People don't do things like that.'

'They do!' George said. 'They do! Quick, pour a kettle of hot water down the plughole and make the horrible people go away.'

'All right, maybe a few people do nasty things, the ones who don't know any better. But that doesn't mean that *all* people are nasty. I mean, some spiders are nasty too, George. But we're not, are we? We don't go crawling up people's trouser legs and frightening them, do we?'

'No – I suppose not,' George agreed.

'Just try not to think about it,' his mum said.

'I'll try,' George said.

But it wasn't easy. It wasn't easy *not* to think of something at all. For the more you tried not to think of it, the more you did.

When George's dad came home from his web-building business, George's mum told him what had happened that afternoon, and he decided it was time that he and George had a talk.

'Tell me what the problem is, George,' he said. 'What is it you don't like about people? Why do they frighten you so much, do you think?'

'Well, first, it's their legs,' George said. 'They've only got two, Dad! They look so strange and creepy they give me the shudders.'

'But, George,' his dad said, 'not everyone has eight legs like us, you know. Why, ladybirds, they only have six legs. And cats, they just have four. And a snail I saw this morning, why, she only had a foot, and the worm that she was talking to had simply no legs at all. And then, on the other side of the coin, there's a millipede out in the garden who has so many legs, he can't even count them all. Because by the time he's counted the ones he's got, he's gone and grown some new ones.'

'Yes, I suppose so,' George said. 'But it's not just that, Dad.'

123

'What else then?'

'Well, their legs aren't properly hairy. Not like ours. Not like yours and mine and Mum's. Why, Mum's got really nice hairy legs. And it's what they eat too.'

'What people eat, you mean?'

'Yes,' said George. 'They don't eat proper food, do they, not like flies. They have things like chips and fish fingers! Eeeech! I mean, just imagine it, Dad, fish fingers. It's enough to make you ill.'

'Yes, I can see what you're getting at, George, and I take your point,' his dad said. 'But you have to remember that different creatures like to eat different things. And it would never do if we all ate the same food, as there might not be enough to go round. Why, if people lived on flies, the same as we do, they'd scoff the lot and we'd have none. But I agree with you that chips do sound disgusting, and there's nothing I like better myself than a big juicy fly. Flies for breakfast, gnats for tea, and a nice bluebottle sandwich in my lunch box, with a daddy longlegs for afters. But we have to live and let live. And though fish fingers and chips might seem strange to us, to other creatures, nothing could be nicer.'

'Yes, Dad, but –' George tried to say, but it was hard to get a word in once his dad had got going.

'Why, a dog I knew once,' Dad went on, 'when I

used to have a web out by the water barrel – I was a single spider in those days, this was before I met your mother – why that dog he liked nothing better than a bone. And a sheep of my acquaintance, she was very fond of grass. Now grass isn't my cup of tea, in fact, I don't like cups of tea at all. I much prefer a dew drop, or a spot of rain on a leaf. And –'

'Yes, I know, Dad,' George said. 'But it's not just that, it's the way people stand on the *floor*, instead of living halfway up the wall, or dangling from the ceiling, like they ought to. They just don't know how to behave or have any manners at all.'

'Hmm, maybe so,' Dad said. 'But what you have to remember is that often, people are just as afraid of spiders as spiders are of people.'

'Yes, Dad,' George said. 'If you say so.' But he didn't really believe it.

Because how could a person be afraid of a spider? People were huge, and spiders were tiny, even the biggest of them was nowhere near the size of a person. People couldn't be afraid of spiders, could they? Especially of ones as small as George, who wasn't even big enough yet to catch flies.

It was ridiculous. He couldn't believe that.

But that night, George woke again with the horrors, and his mum had to go and comfort him.

'There's a person in the wardrobe!' he said. 'And it's coming to get me!'

'Oh, George,' his mum said, opening up the wardrobe door, so that he could see there was nothing there. 'What are we going to do with you!'

And it was ages before he could get back to sleep. His mum had to stay with him, singing him spider lullabyes called Spiderbyes, and telling him his favourite stories, such as 'Spider in Boots', 'Rumple-spider-skin', 'The Spider and the Pea', and 'The Spider's New Clothes'. And it was only after she had told him the story of 'The Spider and the Seven Dwarfs' and had sung him 'Rudolph the Red-nosed-Spider' – both of which were his favourites – that he finally went to sleep.

Now things could have gone on for ever like this, and Spider George might have remained frightened of people for the rest of his life, had he not run into another George – George the boy.

Spider George had gone off exploring in the garden, and he had found himself by a wall. Now, in the wall was a drainpipe. And as George was a curious spider, and as no one had told him not to, he decided to crawl up the drainpipe to investigate, and to see what he might discover.

At first, everything was in darkness, and George became afraid that he might meet something nasty coming the other way. But then he saw some light, at the far end of the tunnel, and he headed for it, to see what might be there. On he went, climbing upwards, finally to emerge from the top of the pipe into what seemed like a great big empty swimming pool, which had been drained of water.

George looked up then, and just above his head he saw two of the most enormous taps he had ever seen in his life. But he recognized them at once, and he scurried up to have a good look at them, and just as he had expected, one of the taps was marked with the letter H for Hot, and the other was marked with the letter C for Cold. And standing next to the taps, in a huge dish, was the largest cake of soap he had ever come across.

It's a bath! George thought. I'm in the bath. I've come up the plughole. But what sort of creature could have a bath like this? It must be the biggest spider in the world to have a bath this size. It must be the greatest spider ever seen. He went for a walk around. Yes, it must be king of all the spiders! The emperor, even! Or maybe it's a giant spider, as in Incy and the Beanstalk, or maybe – but then a chilling, terrifying thought came into his head – maybe this bath belongs to – a PERSON!

As soon as the thought came into his mind, George leaped down from the side of the bath and made a run for the plughole, so as to get back down the drainpipe, as quickly as he could.

He must have been half way there when he heard a noise. He glanced up to see the bathroom door opening, but he didn't stop running.

Then he heard a voice, a great booming voice that stopped him in his tracks.

'George –' the voice said, and for a moment George thought that the voice was talking to him. But then he realized that it wasn't talking to him at all. It was talking to a boy who had just come into the bathroom. A boy with the same name as himself.

'George!!' the great voice boomed – at least it sounded like a great voice to a spider, though to a person, it probably sounded quite ordinary. 'Go and get ready for your bath please. I'll be in to run it in a minute.'

And of course Spider George knew then that the voice belonged to the boy's mother.

He ran as fast as he could to get to the plughole before he was seen. But he wasn't quick enough. A shadow fell over the bath, and George stopped in his tracks, frozen with fear.

This was it.

His worst nightmare.

All his bad dreams come true.

It was –

– a person!

Coming to get him.

George looked up. He saw two big eyes looking down at him. Not nice kind spider's eyes either. But big, bulgy person's eyes. They may have only been a child's eyes, but they looked big to a spider, just the same.

For a second George was too afraid to move, too afraid to scream. This was it. It was going to happen. The boy was going to pick him up and pull his legs off. This was the end. George braced himself for it.

If only my mum and dad were here to save me, he thought. But he was on his own.

And then, a most curious thing happened. Instead of picking him up and pulling his legs off, the boy just stood there for a moment frozen, just as George was frozen, and seemingly unable to move.

Then slowly the boy moved his hand, and he pointed at George with his finger, and he uttered the one word.

'Spider!' he said.

And he yelled so loudly that the soap dish fell off the side of the bath.

George was puzzled.

Spider? he thought. Where's the spider? That boy seems to be afraid of a spider somewhere. I wonder where it is? It must be a pretty big spider to frighten a boy like that.

And George looked around to see where the big spider was, the one that frightened the boy so much, but there was none to be seen.

The boy was yelling very loudly now. And not only was he yelling, he was jumping up and down, and even starting to cry.

'Spider! Spider!' he yelled. 'Mum, Mum! Come quick! There's a spider in the bath!'

Spider George heard footsteps hurrying, and a voice saying, 'Oh, George, not again!' And when he looked up, it was now to see two pairs of bulgy eye-balls looking down at him. There was the big pair and an even bigger pair as well, which seemed to be hidden behind two windows.

Good heavens, thought George. That must be that boy's mother. And look, she's got her own windows! I've never seen a person with their own windows to look out of before. How amazing. Why, if that boy's mother has got windows, then she must be a house. Fancy having a house for your mum. How amazing.

'Spider! Spider!' the boy kept shouting. 'There's a spider in the bath!'

When George heard the boy going on shouting like this, he began to feel rather important.

If I'm so small, and a big chap like that is afraid of me, he thought, I must be more special than I look!

And out of sheer devilment, he puffed himself up to his full size, and he tried to growl and to look fierce, and he showed all his teeth at once, in the hope that he might make the boy even more frightened, and then frighten his mother as well.

'Spider! Spider!' the boy said. 'Nasty spider in the bath!'

But George wasn't able to frighten the boy's mother too.

'Oh, honestly,' she said. 'That's nothing to be afraid of. A tiny little thing like that!'

'It'll run up my trousers,' the boy said. 'And bite me on the bottom.'

'Oh, really, don't be so silly. It's a harmless little spider, that's all.'

Harmless? thought George. Not me. I'm rough and tough and dangerous through and through.

'Kill it!' the boy said. 'Squash it with a newspaper! Pull its legs off!'

'Certainly not,' his mother said. 'I'll put it out of the window.'

Two huge hands descended then. George ran for the plughole. But he wasn't fast enough and the hands were upon him before he could get there.

It really is the end, George thought, it really is. Goodbye cruel world. It was a short life, but a sweet one. It's a pity I never got a chance to grow up, that's all. Goodbye Mum, goodbye Dad, goodbye all the flies I never ate. I knew it would happen. My worst dream has come true. A person is going to get me!

But to his amazement, the hands neither squashed him nor crushed him nor pulled off his legs. Instead, they very gently scooped him up, and tenderly carried him to the window.

And oddly, George didn't feel afraid.

This person, he thought, isn't afraid of me. And I am not afraid of them. For spiders and people can be friends.

The boy's mother opened the bathroom window, and she dropped George out into the air.

The breeze took him, and he descended on a line of spun silk, and he glided right back down to where he had started. And when he landed, he saw his own mother waiting there for him.

'George,' she said, 'I've been looking for you. I wondered where you had gone.'

George told his mother nothing about his adventures. He kept them to himself as his own personal secret. For children come to an age when they don't want to tell their parents everything, and they wish to have private things for themselves.

His mother did notice something different about him though, and she remarked on it to George's father some days later.

'You know,' she said, 'George seems to have stopped having bad dreams. He hasn't woken up in the night for ages. He doesn't seem to have nightmares any more or worry about people coming to get him. I wonder why that is.'

'It's probably the little chat I had with him,' George's father said. 'It must have put his mind at rest.'

And he felt rather pleased with himself that he had solved the problem of George's nightmares.

As for George, he slept as soundly as a log. He was no longer afraid of people, and he hoped that they would no longer be afraid of him. But as he got older, sometimes, out of pure mischief, George would creep up on a little girl or a little boy, and he would go 'Boo!' And he would roll his eyes and waggle all his legs at once, and show all of his teeth. And nine times out of ten, the little boy or the little girl would scream and run away, shouting, 'Ahhh! Ahhh! It's a spider!'

And when they did this, George would laugh, and laugh, and laugh, until the tears ran down his face, and down over his eight hairy legs.

For, to this day, he still can't understand why something as big as a person should be afraid of something as small as a spider.

But it does make him laugh.

And it does make him wonder.

And one thing is for certain – he isn't frightened of people any more.

And he never will be again.

Acknowledgements

The editor and publishers gratefully acknowledge the following, for permission to reproduce copyright material in this anthology.

'The Farmer and the Goddess' by Rosalind Kerven from *In the Court of the Jade Emperor* published by Cambridge University Press 1993, copyright © Rosalind Kerven, 1993, reprinted by permission of Cambridge University Press.

'The Twelve Labours of Heracles' retold by Geraldine McCaughrean from *The Orchard Book of Greek Myths* first published by Orchard Books, a division of the Watts Publishing Group Ltd, 96 Leonard Street, London EC2A 4XD, 1992, copyright © Geraldine McCaughrean 1992, reprinted by permission of Orchard Books.

'The Bag of Winds' retold by Pomme Clayton from *The Orchard Book of Stories from the Seven Seas* first published by Orchard Books, a division of the Watts Publishing Group Ltd, 96 Leonard Street, London EC2A 4XD, 1996, copyright © Pomme Clayton 1996, reprinted by permission of Orchard Books.

135

'How the Badger Got Its Stripes' by Terry Jones from *Fantastic Stories* published by Pavilion 1992, copyright © Terry Jones 1992, reprinted by permission of Pavilion.

'Send Three and Fourpence We Are Going to a Dance' by Jan Mark from *Nothing To Be Afraid Of* published by Hamish Hamilton 1987, copyright © Jan Mark, 1987.

'The Mouth-Organ Boys' by James Berry from *A Thief in the Village* published by Hamish Hamilton 1987, copyright © James Berry, 1987.

'You're Late, Dad' by Tony Bradman from *You're Late, Dad* first published by Methuen Children's Books 1989, copyright © Tony Bradman 1989, reproduced by permission of The Agency (London) Ltd. All rights reserved and enquiries to The Agency (London) Ltd, 24 Pottery Lane, London W11 4LZ. Fax: 0207 727 9037.

'What's in a Name?' by Mary Ross from *Good Sports! A Bag of Sports Stories* edited by Tony Bradman, first published by Corgi 1992, copyright © Mary Ross 1992, reprinted by permission of Laurence Pollinger Limited on behalf of the Estate of Muriel Mary Ross.

Acknowledgements

'Leaf Magic' from *Leaf Magic and Five other Favourites* by Margaret Mahy, published by JM Dent 1977, copyright © Margaret Mahy 1977, reprinted by permission of The Orion Publishing Group Ltd.

'Helping Hercules' by Francesca Simon from *Time Watch* edited by Wendy Cooling, published by The Orion Publishing Group Ltd 1997, copyright © Francesca Simon, 1997, reprinted by permission of The Orion Publishing Group Ltd.

'Spider George' by Alex Shearer from *Side Splitters* edited by Wendy Cooling, published by The Orion Publishing Group Ltd 1997, copyright © Alex Shearer, 1997, reprinted by permission of The Orion Publishing Group Ltd.

'Kylie and the Can-Can Beans' by Caroline Pitcher from *Surprise Surprise* edited by Wendy Cooling, published by The Orion Publishing Group Ltd 1997, copyright © Caroline Pitcher, reprinted by permission of The Orion Publishing Group Ltd.